MW00625624

A LOOK INSIDE A
MANGLED MIND

VOLUME ONE

Serial killers that will stop your heart
leaving raw your mind…and soul,
and other stories by

George Gross III

Cover art by Andrew Caynon

DEDICATION

I would first like to thank my parents for their encouragement to read, to write and to use my imagination without boundaries. They also bought me my first word processor so that I wouldn't have to re-type everything again on that small portable manual typewriter. Also, I would like to thank my sisters for having always believed in me. My older sister and brother-in-law, both having served a long time in the medical field, were called at all hours to get their guidance in keeping the sickness real and believable.

I would also like to thank my editor Scott, for the many years and hours spent reducing my errors to acceptable limits.

I would be remiss if I didn't mention the artist, Andrew Caynon, who took my idea for the cover art and made it a reality better than I could have hoped for.

Lastly, and most importantly, I would like to thank the love of my life, my wife, and our son, for allowing me to follow this dream, for sacrificing the many hours of what could have been quality time together so that I could pursue this endeavor locked away in my cave at my desk. Without their support, this collection and the things to come would not be.

Contents

My Summer Vacation

It took four train rides, nine interstate bus rides, fourteen cab rides, and three weeks to get to where I was standing. Standing there staring, trying to decide what the pattern on the wall resembled. Was it a butterfly caught in the rain? Maybe it was an eagle lifting off from a stream with a trout in its claws? Or was it simply what it was, part of a scalp and high velocity blood spatter on the off-white wall? I was also standing there thinking that it would be a bitch to cover that up. No matter how well you washed it or repainted it, blood seemed to find a way to seep through. That section of the wall would have to be replaced. *Oh well, back to work.*

There was still a light trail of smoke drifting up from the gun barrel and from the hole in the back of the man's head. The bullet had entered just below the right eye and exited high on the left side, behind the ear. I hadn't wanted it to end this way, but he wouldn't stop that incessant screaming. The duct tape muffled it a little, but it was driving me crazy and making it hard for me to concentrate on the work I was trying to perform.

I had inserted an IV drip into his left arm to keep his fluids up as I operated on the right side. Even with the tourniquet, there was a puddle of blood drying under the chair that I had him strapped to. The IV contained a saline/morphine combination that I was hoping would keep him sedated enough to do it right, but apparently it didn't work as well as I had hoped. Now it turns out that he cost me an IV solution for nothing. His screaming started right after the first incision and continued for almost twenty minutes before I shot him, to put him out of my misery. Now at least I could finish this first part in peace. I caught a whiff of something foul. His sphincter and bladder had let go in death. Just one more thing for me to have to clean up later.

"Shit," I said, stepping back. I couldn't continue with this operation. He had to be alive or she would die. What a fucking waste. I had to regain control of the situation and my emotions, so I stepped back and lit up a cigarette, and seeing the blood on my fingers sucked it off before wiping them on my pants leg. I poured a cup of coffee from the twelve-cup drip maker, and walked out onto the back deck. This cabin overlooked a very large lake. There were many other cabins surrounding it, but this weekend was the weekend after Labor Day and most of the residents had gone home to work and start school like good Americans. I had called the principal of the school I worked yesterday and told him that I would be back a week late due to a family emergency. I could do that. I tenure. My high school English Lit class would miss me, but they would be fine until I got back. Months of thought had gone into this and I just about blew it in the first few hours. How stupid.

The smoke burned my throat and the coffee eased my insides. I closed my eyes hoping to see the vision that drove me onward, but all I could think about were the trains, their smell, and all the people. I was also thinking about how I had to suffer all those many hours in their presence. The buses weren't any better. Some shit-for-brains kid had thrown up on one of them and that sour, putrid smell surrounded all of us for the entire sixteen-hour leg of my journey. The only decent part of the whole trip was the three-day hike through the National Forest Reserve to get to this lake. I had entered from the protected side. This lake had roads and homes on three sides allowing for traffic, bicycles and lonely fishermen. Now that Labor Day had past, there were maybe a dozen locals still living here, but none of them lived within a mile walking distance.

I had anticipated finding four victims here, but instead I had gotten lucky and found five. Maybe I could rethink my plan a little and make do with what I had. The father might not be the loss I was envisioning just a moment ago. I had wanted them alive to feel the changes I had in store for them. After all, anyone could carve and do things to a cadaver, but to do those same things to the living.....? I tell my students all the time... 'Preparation, practice and a concerted effort could overcome all sorts of obstacles.' Now, I had to show them how to do just that. I had the mother, the fifteen-year-old son, his fifteen-year-old girl friend who I hadn't considered in this, and of course the twelve-year-old daughter. *What to do? What to do?*

I dropped the cigarette butt onto the deck and stomped it out. Didn't want to inadvertently start a forest fire now did I? The coffee was cooling, and I swallowed the last of it in one huge mouthful. I passed through the kitchen and placed the cup on the counter. I now knew that I needed a second person. I needed an anesthesiologist. Not having one I would have to improvise. I dug through my backpack and found the four vials of the drug Propofol. That should be enough. I would just have to monitor them a little more closely but knocking them out would definitely help with the screaming part anyway.

I dragged the father, still tied to the chair, down the hall into the now empty back bedroom and closed the door. Reaching into the bathroom, I pulled a towel from the rack, dropped it on the floor and used my feet to push it across the bloody area so that I wouldn't slip and fall in it later. Wouldn't want to hurt myself, remember, safety first.

*　　　　　*　　　　　*　　　　　*

I walked into the main bedroom and looked at the four secured people left. The three kids were scared and were trying to hide behind the mother. They all had snot bubbles trailing from their noses and dripping onto their shirts. The mother was looking at me hard, her eyes trying to rip my heart out. They all had heard the gunshot and knew that the father was dead and wouldn't be back to help them. I quickly decided on the girlfriend, grabbed her by the legs and started dragging her out of the room. The son tried to stop me by inch-worming his way over, trying to add his weight. I laughed and pulled her right out from under him and kicked the door shut. When I got to the kitchen, I left her crying on the floor for a moment and pushed everything off of the table, clearing it. I gently picked her up and placed her across its polished wooden surface.

I set up a new IV bag and hooked her up to it. She had good veins and the catheter went in smoothly. Having the IV drip and the syringe, I needed to have a 'smart set' arrangement. That was a very popular 'y' style set up that allowed you to administer syringe drugs while the IV was going, because of the one-way valves it contained. She was trying to hide inside her head with eyes squeezed shut. I knew for a fact that she wasn't even close to thinking about what I was going to do to her. I pulled a syringe full of the Propofol and stuck it into the prepared tubing. I smiled at her closed eyes and depressed the syringe pushing a small amount of the drug into her. In moments her body relaxed, her eyes rolled up and her breathing became deep and constant. I placed a blood pressure cuff on her right arm and checked. It read eighty, over forty-five, perfect. I used the kitchen scissors to remove all of her clothing and tossed them into the corner of the room. Good to go.

*   *   *   *

I was in college, acing all my main courses, when an idea hit me. From that time on I had read and studied as many surgical books as I could get my hands on. I also needed to practice and must say that driving around the countryside is an easy way to find many a stray dog or cat that would jump willingly into your car having tasted some food and smelled more inside. People aren't much smarter. The animals were euthanized and opened. I learned how to use the tools of the trade. How each part of the body reacted to the scalpel and how each of them felt; the muscles, tendons, ligaments, all of the internal organs and of course the skin. I went on to learn how to operate on the living animals, keeping them alive through the horrors of re-arranging their bodies. I could describe it all to you given the time, but right now I am in the middle of something and have to get back at it.

*   *   *   *

It came down to this. How should I attach them?

The scalpel slid easily down her sternum, across her stomach, and all the way to her slightly concave bellybutton, leaving an oozing, widening trail of blood. I then added the typical across the body incisions allowing me to expose the ribcage. I peeled the skin back, watching for signs of discomfort. Her young ample breasts added just the right amount of weight to help hold the skin back and open. Pressing a finger hard between her ribs I felt her young strong heartbeat vibrating up my arm. I made two more small incisions along the breastbone where I would be binding her later. I stopped to check her vital signs and finding them a little erratic I pushed in a few more cc's of the Propofol and watched as they leveled off nicely. I made a deep cut horizontally across her abdomen, like for a c-section. Reaching in, I slowly disconnected her vagina from the internal holdings until I could turn it inside out and ease it out of her. She was ready. Now, for her partner.

I made my way to the bedroom and pushed through the door. I was almost knocked down by the son as he shoved hard against the back of the door. My head hit the door jamb and pissed me off. I turned and punched him hard right on the end of the nose. We all heard the loud crack as it broke and watched as his blood gushed out all down the front of him. He fell back onto the floor and tried to get away from me. The mother leaned forward as if to protect him. I smiled at her. He squirmed over to her and pressed the side of his face against her leg.

"That was just plain stupid," I said while rubbing the side of my head. "Did you really think that through? That was best that the three of you could come up with? Hell, you didn't even try to get the tape off." I was watching the little one to see her reaction. "What was your next trick? To sit on me while one of you rolled for help?" I was laughing by this time and they were just watching me and waiting for what I planned to do to them.

I looked at the son and asked him, "Do you want to come easily, or are you going to make me have to work on you some more?"

He started squirming further away and the mother tried to stand and block my way. I pushed her back on to the bed. I got a hold of him and started dragging him away. He was bucking and struggling. *See, I told you they weren't smarter than the animals.* I let him go and walked out. In a moment I returned with a second syringe of the Propofol. I grabbed him and

8

injected some of the drug right into the vein jumping on his arm. It took less than ten seconds for him to go limp. The mother was screaming again as I pulled the limp boy from the room and closed the door behind me.

I lay him on the table next to the girl and proceeded to cut his clothes off as well, tossing them aside to join the others. I set his IV up exactly like I did for the girl. I checked his vitals and eased in a few more cc's of the drug. He was ready.

As with the girl I started at the top of his sternum and opened him up to the navel. After few horizontal cuts I was peeling back his chest to expose the bones beneath. I made matching incisions along his breastbone as I did with her. Now for the hard part, and I was hoping it would work. I had never tried this before. I used a small piece of latex tubing and made a quick cock ring for him. Playing with his penis and balls I waited until his penis grew hard. Perfect.

The table I was using was wide. I took a moment and propped the girlfriend up onto her left side to face the boy. I used some of the clothes to hold her there. I propped him up on his right side to face her. I checked both of their signs and after finding out they were fine, I continued. I gently rocked him into position and started by sewing his cockhead to the base of her inside out vagina. Pushing them slowly together I stitched her to his shaft as it slowly disappeared inside of her. When I had them tight I made a nice circuit around where they met to seal them together. I stopped and wiped some sweat from my forehead, stepped back and lit a cigarette to get my mind back to where I needed it right now.

I had to work fast but smartly. I took one last drag, tossed the butt into the kitchen sink and turned back to my young couple. I took a moment and checked their vital signs and to give each another quick dose of the Propofol. I reached into my bag and pulled out a coil of stainless-steel wire use for wiring jaws shut. I slowly opened it. Keeping a slight pressure on his back I reached between them and used the wire to lace the breast bones together. I made sure each loop was snug and wrapped in a way to not come loose. I made five complete coils in both of the incisions. That ought to do nicely.

Using their skin flaps and trying to keep their nipples intact I started trimming and stitching them together. I didn't want to leave them with massive scarring, so I used a nice fine silk thread used in facial reconstruction. It took longer than I had anticipated, and I noticed that she was starting to come around. I quickly increased her dosage and waited for her breathing and rhythm to get back to normal. When I had them sealed, I got another image…them kissing. I moved to their faces and slowly stitched their lips together. I made it all around the perimeter with no gaps, an everlasting kiss.

*   *   *   *

A kiss. A kiss that I should have gotten fourteen years ago. Is that why I am here now? Is that what drove me to this? I was suddenly shifted through time to when my life changed. It was three weeks before graduation. An English Professor gave me, wrongly I might add, a B- on a paper. Was he kidding?

I busted my ass on that thing, and for what. He didn't get it. Not only that, but that miserable B- knocked me from being the class Valedictorian to fourth overall. That shift in position closed doors to me. I heard and watched them shut. People looked at me differently and there was nothing I could do about it. I was a failure. A kiss I should have gotten for that honor was taken from me. From that moment on I struggled. I hopelessly watched as positions, and raises that were rightfully mine, were taken from me. That bastard! He shouldn't have screamed so much, and he would still be here, instead of sitting in the back room with smoke leaking out of his head.

*　　　　*　　　　*　　　　*

The moan brought me back to reality. I rushed to them and saw that they needed more dosing, so I did it, moving between them making sure that they were both comfortable before moving on. I opened the refrigerator and found a cold soft drink, popped the top, and drank most of it down on the first few swigs. I lit a cigarette, having tossed the last one away early a few minutes ago. I looked up at the rooster clock on the wall. *Wow,* that was well over four hours ago, *boy did that time go quickly.* I dropped down onto one of the kitchen chairs to rest my legs and finish the soda. *Almost done,* I told myself. I took a long drag on the cigarette and slowly let out the smoke, watching as it made its way towards the ceiling. I was tired, but knew I couldn't stop before I was through with them all. I closed my eyes and took another drag. Letting it out, I thought about all the things I probably should have let out. Anger, disappointment, even the hatred, but I guess it is too late for any of that now. Almost done here, and I did learn a few things for next time. I took one last drag and dropped the butt into the almost empty can which I set on the kitchen counter behind me.

I checked the two teenagers on the table, making sure that everything was fine before I headed in to get the mother. I grabbed a syringe of the anesthesia on the way for the girl. Opening the door to the room I got a shock. The mother had most of her restraints off and was trying to get out of the window. She turned around and launched herself at me. I grabbed her, but in her wild state she was hard to hold. She was kicking and punching, and I was getting hurt. I punched her in the face, and she staggered back out into the hallway. She turned and ran towards the kitchen with me hot on her heels. When she turned the corner, she stopped dead and a scream like nothing I had ever heard filled the room. She was standing there looking at the two children on the table. I walked up and injected her with the Propofol and helped her to the floor as it took effect.

I took a moment to check over my injuries. There was a swelling under my left eye where she had caught me good and both shins were starting to bruise. I left her there to go look for the girl. She wasn't in the room and after searching, wasn't in the house anymore either. *Shit,* the window. I ran outside and started looking around for signs of her. I was running in every direction when I heard her. A soft crying was coming from off to my left. I closed in on the sound and found her sitting behind a tree holding her head in her hands and trying not to cry. I knelt next to her and she tightened up into a ball. I pulled her close and slipped the syringe into her thigh. She didn't scream, she just sat there and slowly slipped into unconsciousness. I picked her up and made my way back into the house. I lay her on the couch where I could keep an eye on her.

I went to the kitchen sink and washed my hands and face to clean them, and to cool off from all of the exertion of the last five minutes. I dried my hands and checked on all of my subjects. They all seemed ok. I slid the mother across the floor and hoisted her up onto the table, and like the others proceeded to cut off all of her clothes. She was a good-looking woman for her age and had nice smooth skin. Her breasts, from having children, had started to sag a bit, but were still very nice. I took a moment to appreciate them before moving on. I checked her signs and upped her dose just a bit more, not knowing how much got in there the first time. I went and picked up the girl and placed her next to her mother on the table. I wanted the look to be just right. I removed her clothing and checked her signs. They were ready. Taking a magic marker out of my bag, I placed the mother's arms around the girl. I made marks where they over lapped. I did the same with the girl. Taking each arm in turn, I slowly cut around them at each of the marks and removed the skin from those areas.

When all four were done, I moved to their sides. I had to guess a little for the size, but I made long incisions on the mother's side and tried it out. I slowly shoved my hand into the back cut and pushed it through, wiggling my fingers back and forth to break the skin's adhesion to the fatty layers. When my hand finally made it out of the front slice, I took the girl's hand in mine and pulled it back through the hole I had just made. When it was in place, I checked my measurements and found them to be close enough. I sewed the girls forearm skin to the mothers back and upper arm to the front. This was going to take some time. I took a moment to check the vital signs for all four people on the table and adjusted the dosage as I thought fit.

I had messed up a little here. I should have fed the mother's arm through the hole in her daughter before stitching the girl's arm down. It took some pushing and shoving, and I almost dropped them on the floor while struggling to get it through. The skin on the girl's front abdomen tore raggedly up towards her chest and I didn't notice that until I started to close it up. *I must remember to pull both arms through before sewing them up.* I did notice though, that my sewing, or stitching, was getting much better. All this practice and I would put my closures up against any surgeon now. I started pulling the mother's arm through the girl when I heard a sound. I stopped, stood and waited. Hearing nothing for over a minute, I continued pulling the mother's arm through the hole and started on the girl's arm. When they were both interlaced, I stopped again. I definitely heard something this time.

I went to the front door, checked that it was locked and peeked along the edge of the curtains to see if anyone was out front. I saw nothing, so I moved on to the back door and looked out over the back yard. Nothing there either. I stood still and listened. I could hear the kitchen rooster clock. I could hear drips of blood falling from the table into the small puddles underneath. I could hear the wind in the trees out back. I could even hear the faint sound of the water against a boat hull by the dock.

I heard the gunshot right after I felt the searing pain explode in my shoulder. I was knocked forward into the kitchen cabinets and fell backwards over my legs. Standing there was a cop. He was staring at my work on the table. His mouth was moving up and down quickly with no sound coming out. I could also see his stomach churning, trying to lose the lunch it took in a few hours ago. He walked quickly past the table and came up to me. He saw that I was no longer a threat and handcuffed me behind my back.

"Roger," he called over his shoulder, "in here."

"Holy shit!"

That must have been Roger. I was losing my focus as the pain and blood loss was sending me to the dark place. I could hear voices intermittently yelling about paramedics, and helicopters. Just before I died, I could feel my body being lifted.

* * * *

"I didn't die. They fixed me. I still have trouble moving my shoulder up all of the way, but it mostly works. Besides, in here I don't have to lift it at all. Do I Doc?" I asked the doctor who was reviewing my case. He was trying to decide how insane I really was. "You asked me how I came to be here, and I told you. That is the truth about how I spent my summer vacation."

He closed the file, nodded his head, and got up to leave the wardroom.

"Did they survive," I asked?

He turned and looked at me. "The mother and daughter did. They needed extensive surgery and therapy, but they made it. The son and his girlfriend didn't, and you know about the father."

I nodded and he turned and left me without looking back.

Two nice guys wearing white uniforms walked up to the table. One of them took a small package out of his pocket, opened it and used the rubbing alcohol pad in it to prepare my arm for my afternoon meds. They couldn't trust me to take my pills, so I get nothing except injections now. They turned and walked away. I was still laced to the chair and would remain that way until dinner, but I could turn my head to look out of the window.

The blue sky and wispy clouds carry me back to that time in a cabin in the woods and a small smile pulls my lips back. My head feels heavy and I think I need a nap now.

"Good night."

THE END

The First Date

The sweltering heat had me dizzy as I strolled down the lamp-lit alleyway. Melodic jazz strains pulsed through the smog-layered air, pressing against me like a warm overcoat. The half empty red wine bottle hung loosely from my left hand spilling its contents behind me, a slug's trail for all to follow. Above me, past the dirty half-open windows, and past the jagged edge of the splintered brick roofline, the waxing gibbous moon seemed to follow me. It was haunting me down street after street and alleyway after alleyway. It knew.

How did I get to this state? I remember being a happy guy. My memories, trapped in the haze, have twisted their meanings. I had yearnings, passions, wanting's and desires. Images danced before my impaired eyes.

*   *   *   *

She was beautiful. Her eyes, that really light brown, were hypnotic. Perfectly shaped and very kissable lips wetted by a tongue barely showing itself. She and I were eating dinner. We met, and I remember the rain. The afternoon was so dark that it seemed like night due to the oppressive cloud cover. Only a few 'cool' people were still wearing their shades, more to hide their drug or drink reddened eyes than for protection from the non-existent sun. Cars, trucks, buses and people moved quickly and noisily through the haze. A few brave street hawkers still lined the sidewalks hoping for a last-minute sell before the coming rain would wash the customers and their wares, away. The cab dropped me off right out front, but I still got soaked running across the sidewalk to the entrance. There was a 'Please Wait to be Seated' sign, so I did. A pretty young woman dressed all in black and wearing a bright white smile approached, "Table for one?"

"Ah, two, I'm meeting someone," I answered, and she turned and picked up a second leather bound menu.

"Follow me, sir," she said as she turned and lead me to a small table.

"May we please have that table by the window? Our first date and I want this to be just right."

She smiled, "Of course," and placed the menus on the table that I had suggested. "Would you like to start with a drink, or wait for your date?"

"I'll wait, thank you. It shouldn't be long."

I watched as she walked away. *Damn, if I were ten years younger.* I shook the last of the rainwater from my jacket and placed it on the chair next to me and sat down. A waiter soon approached and poured water into my glass, the ice tinkling like a crystal skeleton. I asked that he also pour a second one, as I would be joined shortly. I took a moment to take in my surroundings. The restaurant's lighting was muted, with recessed lamps hidden behind boxed overhangs. There were candles on the tables, adding to the romantic feel, set on real white linen fabric table covers. The napkins, also linen, were folded properly into small pyramids, and I used mine to wipe my glasses. Dark wood chairs and tables, lined up against the chair-rail height paneling that finished the room nicely, were in contrast to the light peach color they had used on the walls, along which were hung, every few feet, original paintings and copies of the masters.

I sipped my water and was just starting to review the menu when I saw a flash of bright red off to my right. I looked up and saw her. *Wow*. She had chosen a bright red, thin-strapped dress that barely dropped below her knees. It fit snuggly to her torso but became billowy as it fell from her shapely hips. Her hair was raven, cut to surround a pretty almond shaped face, and she was in the process of flipping a small piece of it back over her shoulder where it joined the rest. I had only seen pictures of her before and knew that she was beautiful, but I wasn't prepared for this. Stunning was a word that would have come to mind, if mine had been working at the moment. She must have spotted me, because she smiled and started to head towards me. I just sat there mesmerized, probably drooling and watched her move. She could have been a dancer or a gymnast. Either one could move like that and attract every male eye in the room to imagine what it would be like to make love to that woman. And some women were watching too, maybe checking out the competition. I stood to greet her as she approached.

"Hello, Dave, good to finally meet you face to face." It looked like she meant it.

"Same here, Vicky," I responded. She leaned in for a hug and gave me a kiss on the cheek. I realized I should do the same, but just as I turned to do so, she was already retreating and out of reach. She left behind her scent. Not flowery or citrus or musky, it was something different, and it made you want to stop and take a good whiff. I didn't just then, though it was hard not to, it would have been tacky.

Dave, that was me, Dave Conway. I was thirty-two years old with a full head of dirty blonde hair and dark brown eyes. I've never been married because I've been too busy making my way up the career ladder. I work in banking, more accurately, online banking. I am one of a few chosen people at my company that makes the choices of where we spend and invest our money. I say chosen, because this is usually a high turnover position due to the fact that most people end up losing money. I have yet to do that. Some, but not all, of my investments lead the money totals and that is why I am still employed.

She was Vicky Levin. She was thirty-four and as I stated earlier, she was also a looker. She owned her own business downtown. It was an interior decorating firm, but with a twist. Instead of going all uppity for the rich, she found a way to get the masses to spend what little they had for that sort of thing, with her. She told me that her company had done well over seven figures last year. What her company lacked in big jobs, it made up for in quantity. She made the average Joe, and his wife, feel special by giving them the high quality, professional decorating experience on a budget.

As we were sitting down, she asked, "Have you eaten here before?"

"A few times on special occasions, and once or twice with a couple of potential clients. You?"

"No," she said, and left it like that.

When our waiter arrived and asked about drinks, she quickly jumped in, "What about a pitcher of martinis with a lot of olives on the side?"

"Okay with me," I said, sitting back with a smile on my face. I was also thinking that in all the chats and emails, I couldn't recall ever mentioning that I liked martinis. "I must say, Vicky, that you look absolutely stunning tonight."

"Why, thank you, Dave. I ran home and showered after work, hoping that I could catch a cab back up here to meet you on time. A client was giving me a hard time about what they considered off white, as opposed to what I had shown them previously, and then provided. But, enough about work."

Her smile was amazing. I could probably sit here all night just looking at her. The waiter arrived and slowly poured each of us a drink then he set the pitcher down on the side of the table on a velvet covered trivet and backed away. We picked up our glasses and I offered a toast, "To new beginnings."

"Here, here," she said while reaching across the table to clink the edges of our glasses together.

We each took a sip and smiled. The martini was delicious. Vicky used the small plastic sword-like toothpick to spear an olive and place it on her tongue. She rolled it around teasingly before closing her teeth just enough to keep it from popping out when she withdrew the sword.

"I was hoping you weren't going to cancel because of the rain," I told her as we started perusing the menus. "I am also hoping that it will blow over while we are in here so that we'll be able to take a stroll after we eat, if that is okay with you?"

"Sure, that would be nice." She was playing with that toothpick, sort of chewing on it. She was getting me hot. "Sort of makes me wish I had worn sneakers," she added.

I gave the waiter the signal and he came over to take our order. I chose the twelve-ounce filet mignon with a baked potato and baby vegetables. Vicky decided, after conversing with the waiter, on the tuna steak with a side of baked scallops. She also asked for the side salad with raspberry-vinaigrette to top things off. After he retreated with our choices and menus, we got to the point of getting to know each other more.

*　　　　*　　　　*　　　　*

I was tired of the dating scene and the endless nights in discos and noisy clubs. I wasn't finding the type of women I was looking for. I finally took the chance and signed up with one of those 'Fill out the profile and we will match you,' online dating sites. At first, I thought it was crazy. 'Do I like pina coladas? Does nudity offend me? Do tattoos and body piercings turn me off?' So, I was afraid to answer all of the questions totally truthfully. But after weeks of nothing, and worse, I went back and updated the profile to be more accurate. It wasn't long after that, that I received an email from Vicky.

Apparently, she was in the same sort of situation. She had almost gotten married once, but the wedding was cancelled after she found the groom banging his ex-girlfriend. She had tried the clubs and discos too, finding the choice of men there limited to ass holes or jerks. One of her friends had talked her into trying this site after a night of boo-hooing on that friend's couch. That friend, incidentally, was married and doing everything in her power to help Vicky get out of singlehood and into a blissful marriage just like hers. It turns out that she had signed up to the same dating service just a week after I had.

It was three weeks ago that I had answered her email and we were soon sending them a few times every day. Last week I gave her my phone number and asked if she felt comfortable enough to call me. I had barely hit the send button when the phone rang, making me jump. It was her. Her voice sounded good. You could tell that she was educated, and obviously from New York, and that first phone call had lasted more than an hour. We hit it off. We both liked similar movies and authors. Both had spent time at the Met museum staring at the same oils and sculptures. Both liked Huey Lewis, Styx and The Police, but also Coltrane, Miles and Corea. Now, I find out she also likes martinis. It was almost like we were made for each other.

*　　　　*　　　　*　　　　*

The waiter carried our food over on a huge silver carrying tray and placed each dish gently in front of us. Both plates were still steaming, and he advised us to be careful, as the plates would be hot. I thanked him after he had topped off our martinis before he moved away. We were talking about the latest superhero movie that hit the market last weekend as we prepared our food to our liking. I was buttering the potato and adding just a touch of steak sauce to my meat, while she added just a pinch of salt and pepper to the fish and scallops.

"I couldn't wait to see if they made him anything like the comics, or were they going to turn him into a quasi caricature of himself," she was saying as if he was a real person, "but from what the previews show, it just might be good."

"Agreed. It would be terrible if they made him too wussy or phony. Maybe the kids would like it, and that's where all the marketing is centered, but the adults would turn away. Wow, this is a good steak. How's your tuna?"

"Very good, tender, and not too fishy. The salad is also very fresh, I like that. I hate it when they bring out wilted lettuce. No reason for that." She took a mouthful of the tuna and wiped her lips on the napkin.

I wanted to kiss those lips and was debating on how to do just that. Boy, she was beautiful. I couldn't stop looking at her. I was eating and talking, but all that I could think about was that she was with me and how good that felt. I was the envy of every man here tonight. She was laughing.

"I'm sorry, did I miss something?" I asked as she tilted her head at me like a puppy would at a new sound.

"Where were you? I was telling you something and you seemed to just drift off."

"I am so sorry. Honestly, I don't know what happened. We were talking and...what?"

"Are you telling me I am boring you? Or are you lying to me?"

"Vicky, you are in no way boring. I wasn't quite telling the truth, but I wasn't lying."

"Tell me what you were thinking right now, or I'm out of here. I thought you were different."

"I'm sorry. Okay." I put down my knife and fork. "I was watching you eat, and when you wiped your lips, all I could think about was kissing them. How they would feel, and how they would taste. I really didn't mean to zone and didn't realize that I did. I'm sorry."

"Why didn't you?" she asked.

"Didn't what? Kiss you?"

"Yeah."

"I don't know. Fear probably. Listen...."

"Here," she said as she started leaning forward, offering me her lips. I leaned in and kissed her. Not hard, not soft. I felt her kissing me back. Then, those lips were gone.

"How was it?" she asked as she picked up another olive on the sword.

"Very nice and thank you. I'm really sorry that happened. I'm usually better at this," I tried to explain as I picked up my martini.

"Forget it," she said. "How about them Mets?" Her laughter was beautiful, and I joined in.

We finished eating and both ordered the cheesecake and coffee for dessert. The incident was apparently forgotten. When the coffee, which was a very good dark roast, was done and the check paid, we put on our coats and headed for the street. It had stopped raining, but when I asked about the walk, she suggested we just take a cab back to her place. I wasn't one to argue and put up my hand as I smiled down at her. In moments, a yellow cab pulled over, and after taking her address pushed its way back into traffic.

Her apartment was great. It was a large loft on the top floor of a converted warehouse. All of the brickwork and support poles were painted eggshell white. There were colorful wall hangings and bright colored pillows tossed around on the large sectional cream couch. Three large Oriental triptych pieces broke the large room into smaller, more manageable sections.

"Very nice place you have here," I commented. "I just love those sectional dividers."

"Thank you, I found those on a trip to Vancouver, oh, maybe two years ago. They fell off a ship, if you know what I mean." She was entering a side room that appeared to be the kitchen.

"Must be a bummer to heat this area in the winter. Does it get real hot in the summer?"

"Thankfully I don't mind a chill in the air, but yeah, the heating costs are ridiculous. In the summer, I leave the windows open and it develops a strong cross breeze that keeps it actually pretty nice." She was opening a bottle of wine to pour into the two crystal glasses on the counter.

"Wow, I like this painting here. Who is it?"

"Which one?"

"The lone character standing on the mountain top with the sun climbing behind him. There is something about it that just draws me in."

"I don't know who it is. I found that one at an estate sale just after I opened the business. I couldn't let it go." She came walking in without her heels on, and that was when I noticed that she was wearing stockings. She was balancing the two drinks in one hand and playing with a remote in the other. "There it is." Music broke the silence. I recognized it as an early Miles Davis cd.

"Nice choice," I said as she handed me my wine. She smiled and started dancing across the polished wooden floor. I stood there watching her.

Out of the corner of my eye I noticed a painting of a martini glass surrounded by dancing olives and strawberries. It had a very dramatic presentation, bold colors and high contrast. Some of the olives had pimentos in them and some were wearing high heels. I liked it. As she danced, she was removing her dress. It took a while for me to notice it because she was being so subtle. Hiking it up a little on this pass and nudging it slightly off the shoulder when she spun back around. She was kicking it to the side when she saw me admiring her with a slight smile on my face.

"You like?"

"Oh yeah. What's not to like?" She was wearing a silk and lace bra and matching panties out of one of those popular lingerie catalogs. She was also wearing a garter belt that matched them, and which was holding up the black stockings I was leering at earlier.

She approached me, and after setting her wine on one of the end tables, grabbed me and planted a nice long kiss on my hungry lips. I returned it, and found her tongue joining mine. She was pulling me, and I was following. I would follow her anywhere she wanted to go.

Everything in this new room was white, bright white, except for the curtains, which were black. The large, floor to ceiling windows were open and a breeze was making the curtains dance in and out, rising and falling like ocean waves. In the center of the room was a small bed. There would be no way to lose your partner on this thing. It would also be almost as hard to get away from them even if you wanted too. And right now, I didn't want to. She sat on the edge of the bed and started undressing me. When I tried to unbutton my shirt, she pushed my hands away. I let her do what she needed to do.

My clothes were slowly disappearing and were forming a pile near the end of the bed. I was soon naked. She rose from the bed and turned me to sit on it.

"Vicky, I......." she stopped me by putting her finger to my lips.

"Shhhhhh." She started by removing the bra, then the panties. She left the garter and stockings on. There was a lump in my throat as I took her in. The only light in the room was moonlight that shone through the above skylight sending our dark shadows dancing around the room. She gently pushed me back to lie down and then climbed up to straddle me. Leaning over me, she kissed my forehead, then my nose, and then placed a passionate kiss on my lips. I pulled her to me with no resistance.

We made love for what seemed an eternity. We took our time getting to know each other's bodies. How we reacted to certain things and not to others. Our lips and fingers and hands and limbs all had minds of their own. We climaxed together more than once and finally fell, covered with sweat to each other's side, and lay there breathing deeply. I was trying to understand what this was all about. I remember starting to doze while my fingers were running through her hair, watching her sleep.

I was thinking that she might be the one. She seems so right for me in so many ways. I guess those dating service ads were right. I was thinking about tomorrow, the weekend and what I would like to do with her. So many places to go, and more things to see and do. Thinking about.....

I woke up to an empty bed. It was still dark outside, and the moon light was shining on the far wall. I must not have been out long. I got up and started looking for Vicky, picking up my wine glass to sip the remnants. She was gone. The apartment was empty. I went back to the bed and started getting dressed, picking up my folded clothes, remembering the care Vicky had taken in placing them there. When I was dressed, I walked to the kitchen to place my glass in her sink. There, leaning on the open wine bottle, was a note.

'Dave. I'm sorry to have left you like that, but it is better that we never see each other again. The people, whose apartment that is, will be home in the afternoon so you have some time to leave...' I was dumbfounded. I couldn't believe what I was reading... 'You are a nice guy and someday I'm sure that you'll find the right woman, who will appreciate all that you have to offer. I had a great time tonight and will think of you often. Vicky'

Holy shit. Who was this woman? Was her name even Vicky? I picked up the rest of my belongings and closed the door behind me. When I hit the curb, the rain was coming down again and there were no cabs to be seen. I started heading north towards my place. My mind was racing. How could this have happened? She was perfect. A few blocks later I came across an open pub and climbed up on one of its empty bar stools to figure this out.

*　　　　*　　　　*　　　　*

Images of red dresses and garters flashed before my eyes. Images of tiny dancing olives, some in heels, were mocking me from my peripheral vision. A white room with curtains blowing on hot breezes, dark curtains....black curtains. Silhouettes of bodies were meshing on a silk strewn futon, their limbs appearing and disappearing as they rolled and turned over in the moonlight.

I stumble and fall against a wall, the carbon etched bricks making their mark on my clothes and skin. Sitting, I take a big gulp of the warming grape juice, the low-cost liquid burning my mouth and throat as it makes its way to the brain. The people in my head driving me crazy couldn't be this woman and me. We've just met. I don't know anymore. One more wet sip and the empty bottle clanks its way across the alley to fall silent against the stinking detritus. A howl escapes me, scaring both human and non-human alike. The humans crossed the street to give the alley a wide berth. The animals, I could hear them scrambling to get away into the dark shadows that lined the area. Alone I cried.

*   *   *   *

I awake to the 'You've got mail' tone on the computer in front of me. Startled, I look around. The alley, the moon, the stink, and the wine felt so real. The taste in my mouth was sour and overpowering. Emotionally spent, I laugh out loud. As I reach for the keyboard, I stop…the dark smudges on my hands…soot from the alley? My pants too show signs of dampness and dirt. Then I remember replacing the ink cartridge in the printer earlier. I laugh again. The woman I dreamt about couldn't be real, right? Think about it. Red dresses and olives….white rooms with black curtains….I should be writing this down. It would make a good story someday.

THE END

Bless me Father

(Detective Matthews - Pt 1)

Oh my God, make it stop! I wanted to call my mommy. The pain shooting up my leg was so intense. *Please, oh please, stop this pain.* In the background I could hear a loud shrieking, someone was screaming insanely, and I wish they would stop that as well.

I opened my eyes and the man with the lifted hammer stepped back from the table and cocked his head to the side like a curious puppy. With his left hand he picked up a rag and shoved it in my mouth. The shrieking stopped abruptly. *Oh God, that was me.* I looked down to see the hammer strike the large spike impaling my ankles not only together but also to the table. A second later the pain exploded in my head. *Why, is this happening to me?* The agony didn't seem to cloud my mind. The screaming was muffled now. Oh yeah, he had put a rag in my mouth. I tried to rise but my chest was very heavy. Tipping my head, a little to the left, I could see the leather strap. I tried pulling my right hand to me, to remove the offending rag, but it didn't come. Turning that way, I could see two sets of straps. One was placed between my shoulder and elbow, the second halfway to the wrist. I could also see the bloody pulp of my hand puffing up around a second spike. Turning to the left, I saw a third making a mess out of that hand as well.

The crisp metal on metal clang of the hammer sent another wave of pain up through my body. The screaming in my head was loud and it wasn't helping one bit at all. *There has to be a reason. This has to be a dream. Yeah, a dream. People don't get crucified in real life. Not anymore, right?* I felt a hand on my arm and opened my eyes again. The man was inserting a syringe. I looked up at him.

"A little morphine to help keep you conscious my friend. Don't want you dying on me just yet."

That voice. I knew that voice. I looked again at the face. *I knew that too, I think.* I was trying to piece it together when the sound of a cell phone broke the silence. The man reached into his pocket, pulled out a phone and flipped it open. By the time he said….

"Hello…"

…I knew who it was. It was….

"…Father Daniels." He smiled down at my wide shocked eyes. He even winked at me. He saw the recognition on my face. "Yes, Miss Patty, what can I do for you?" He retreated a little and shrank down out of sight. There must have been a chair there. "A detective? From the police? What are they looking for?" I could hear him tapping his feet as he spoke. I was also starting to feel warm, like someone was running warm water over me. I guess that was the morphine. "Please tell the Detective that I will be in the office in about a half-hour and that he can come by then. I will make all the time that he needs to see what this is all about. Okay, Miss Patty?" I heard the phone snap shut and the scrape of a chair. I could make out the man's shape, or Father Daniels' shape, as he approached. The pain was receding, but the blackness was growing. "You still with me Bill?" I guess me turning my head in his direction was enough of a response for him. "Do you know who I am, Bill?" I did. "Blink your eyes if you do." I did. "Good, that makes things a little easier doesn't it, Bill? To know who is hurting you, even if you don't know why? I have to run back to the office for a little while, but I will be back later to finish up with you…." Slowly I faded, losing the rest of the conversation. "…..would hate to miss out…."

*　　　　*　　　　*　　　　*

A knock on the door and Father Daniels looked up to see Miss Patty leading in a large well-dressed man. Not large as in overweight, but large as in six-foot four and two hundred and twenty pounds. He looked like someone who should be playing the middle linebacker position for any team in the NFL. He was younger than Father Daniels, who at forty-four was young for a pastor of his own congregation, but not by much.

"Good evening, Father. I hope I am not interrupting you," the detective said with a smile.

"Not at all, Detective…" Father Daniels started while shaking the man's hand.

"Matthews."

"..Detective Matthews. My door is always open to the police to help in any way that I can."

"Good to hear that, Father."

"Would you like some coffee, Detective?" Miss Patty asked, halfway hidden by the door she was holding.

"Only if it is not just for me, Ma'am."

"Yes, Miss Patty, coffee would be nice. Thank you," Father Daniels added.

The door closed almost soundlessly. Father Daniels indicated the leather armchair in front of the desk and the detective moved to it and sat easily. Father Daniels moved around, and sat down, leaning his elbows on the massive century-old desk.

"Kind of late for a priest to be out isn't it, Father?" the detective asked noting the clock on the wall.

"Time doesn't stand still for the working of God, detective. There are needy people all over that need our helping hands all the time. I tell you, there are times there just isn't enough hours in the day." The priest's smile was met by the detectives.

"I understand that."

"Oh, I'm sure you do, detective. The criminals don't punch out at five for you either, do they."

"No, Father, I guess they don't." The detective smiled again at that thought.

With a light knock on the door, Miss Patty entered and placed a tray, containing two cups, spoons, a creamer, a sugar bowl and a coffee carafe on the desk. With a small nod, or bow, the detective couldn't tell which, she faded into the background and closed the door behind her.

As Father Daniels poured, he asked the detective, "So tell me, what brought you here tonight?"

"Well, Father, a missing person."

"A child?"

"No, Father, an adult male. One of your parishioners."

"Oh my," Father Daniels replied while picking up his cup of black coffee. The detective added sugar and cream to his.

"Yes, he's a husband and father of two." The detective sipped from the cup and then placed it down to get his notebook from the breast pocket of his suit. "A Mr. Bill Thompson."

"Bill. Oh, my. Yes, I know Bill. What has happened to him?"

"How well do you know him Father?"

"I have known Bill for many years. He has been in counseling with me recently dealing with some issues."

"What sort of issues, Father?"

"Unfortunately, I cannot tell you that. The sanctity of the confessional and of this office does not allow me to do so."

"Well, Father, that might have to come out sooner or later, if he doesn't show up soon."

"I'm afraid it won't, detective." Father Daniels closed his eyes for a moment in concentration. "I can tell you this though, I am sure that what Bill and I have discussed here has nothing to do with his disappearance. It is not that sort of issue."

"You sure, Father?" the detective paused, and then added, "According to his wife, Bill came to see you Monday evening for a...," he checked his notes, "...seven o'clock appointment. He hasn't been seen since."

"Really? He left here in good spirits as I remember."

"And what time was that, Father? Do you remember?"

"Well, his appointment is for an hour. From seven to eight, but I think he hung around for a few minutes talking about the Giants game. I'm sure it wasn't long, so maybe by eight-fifteen he was leaving."

"Was he hoping the Giants would win?"

"Oh yes, he's a big fan."

"Could he have stopped off at a sports bar on the way home?"

"Oh, detective, I just wouldn't know and couldn't hazard a guess."

"Well, Father, I guess that is all for now. Here is my card if you happen to remember anything. Anything at all."

"Okay, detective. I will. I will also call Sharon. She must be going crazy for these last two nights."

"That wouldn't hurt Father. She seems very upset by his not coming home. She also mentioned that she had called here about it."

"She did?"

"Yes. She told us that at…" Detective Matthews glanced down at his bad handwriting again, "…about ten Monday night. Long after she thought he should have been home."

Father Daniels walked to the door, opened it and asked Miss Patty to come in. "Miss Patty, apparently Bill Thompson didn't go home after he left here Monday night. Do you know anything about that?"

"Well, Father. Mrs. Thompson did call Monday night, late, and asked if he was still here. I told her that he left at the usual time. She asked if he was all right and I told her that he seemed fine when he left. She didn't call back, so I had just assumed that all things worked themselves out. Did I do something wrong?"

"Not at all," the detective said, "you've been a big help. Thank you."

"Is Mr. Thompson okay?"

"Right now, he is missing. We have nothing to think anything bad has happened to him."

"I will say a prayer for his safe return, and for his family. Those little girls of his must be so scared." With that she turned and closed the door again behind her.

"Well, detective. I will definitely do a little praying of my own for Bill and his family. If I think of, or hear anything I will call you right away."

"Thank you, Father. I'm sure he'll turn up. Might just be sleeping it off. The Giants did win after all. Might have had a few too many."

"I would hate to think so, but I guess it is possible."

"I will let you know if we find anything, okay Father."

"Oh yes, please do. I will be worried sick until it is resolved."

The detective left closing the outside door behind him. Father Daniels stood there with his eyes shut listening until he heard the car door close, the engine start, and the clinking of the gravel on the fenders fade as it made its way down the street.

*   *   *   *

I was burning up. Sweat was running down the back of my neck. Pain was throbbing its way back into my head. My shoulders hurt from being held at the side for so long. My back hurt from the hard board I was lying on. My hands and ankles were in excruciating pain that was pounding, pulsing with each heartbeat. I opened my eyes and saw nothing but black. After a moment or two I started making out shapes in the dark. There must be a window nearby and the moon, or a streetlamp was making it not quite pitch black in here.

It looked like there were four…no five…well maybe five other crosses in the room. I couldn't tell if they were occupied or not. *Why was Father Daniels doing this? He seemed like the perfect priest. Calm, loving, honest, and well…priestly.* I was having a hard time wrapping my head around what was happening to me. I had to pee. I tried to forget about it but couldn't. I heard a moan off to my left. *Shit! There is someone else.* I tried to say something, to call out, but the rag in my mouth made it about impossible. I moaned loudly and listened. Nothing. I couldn't quite turn my head far enough to see any better. The spike through my right hand just wouldn't allow it. I couldn't take the pressure anymore, I had to pee badly now. I closed my eyes and let it go. I felt the familiar sensation of release and then the warm flood as it soaked through my underwear and across my body. I felt it pooling under my lower back.

The morphine was wearing off and the persistent pulsing of my wounds was starting to get unbearable. I felt feverish. I could hear sounds in the room, but none of them sounded human. Maybe it was rats. The urine was cooling off and its odor was mixing with the dampness and stench of the room. I hadn't noticed it at first, but this room smelled of death. The rotting corpses hanging on the other crosses would be my guess. I was wondering how long some of them had been here. Days or weeks? Months maybe? *My God. How could someone do this? How could a priest do this?* My mind was going in too many directions. The fear, pain and drugs were making it hard to know reality from panic induced imagination.

I heard the moan again, off to my left. I knew that someone was alive, even if just barely. I tried moaning loudly again to let them know that they weren't alone. Again, I got no response. For the first time since I found myself here, a picture of my wife and daughters flashed across my mind. *Oh shit! What are they going through? What have they been told? Do they think I just ran away from them?* I was scared and pissed off. I could feel tears rising in my eyes, building and then blocking the light. I closed my eyes and sobbed while thinking about how I had let them down.

*　　　　*　　　　*　　　　*

"Bill, Bill." Father Daniels was standing over me. "Had to soil yourself I see. Very child-like, Bill. Did it make you feel better?"

I just stared at him. I must have dozed off for a while. How long? No way to tell. The urine was ice cold against my skin. I could also feel the stickiness of the drying tears on my cheeks. Father Daniels reached down and pulled the rag from between my dried lips.

"Who else is here?" My voice was raspy, and I coughed when I finished asking the question.

Father Daniels looked at me and said, "There are four others. Three are dead and the fourth one…just won't seem to die. He has been here almost two weeks now and I am honestly shocked at his persistence."

"Why are you doing this to me, to us?"

"You should know the answer to that, Bill. You have come to me and confessed your sins on numerous occasions."

"Doesn't that absolve me of my sins?"

"Only if you truly repent, do your penance and never do that sin again. You, however, are a repeat pedophile. One who has not changed his ways and who I am sure will continue. Continue to ruin the lives of those you molest. And let's not forget what this has done to your family, Bill. Do you think Sharon and the girls don't know? They can tell there is something wrong."

He was right. I didn't want to admit it, not even to myself, but he was right. I would continue. Feeling those young girls, their suppleness and their oh so smooth and tender skin. It was irresistible. "But Father, killing us is wrong too, isn't it?"

"Yes, Bill, it is. I have chosen my fate as the sword of God. If he decides that I have done wrong on my judgment day, then I will freely accept his decision. However, I truly believe that I am doing his work, with his guidance."

"Can't you help me change, Father? Stop now and turn me around?"

"Bill, we both know in our hearts that you are lost to us."

"What about my family?"

"They think that you are missing and might have run away. I spoke to Sharon not yet an hour ago and though she is upset at not knowing, she is being strong for the girls. When they find you, in a few weeks, they will be better off. Your life insurance will keep them content for a long time. And Bill, do you think Sharon is still yours?"

"Yes."

"She is lost to you too, Bill. She only stays for the support and for the girls. With you gone, she can move on with her life and not be the adulterer that you are."

"I don't believe you." I tried to get anger to swell my voice, but we both knew how week and unterrifying I was at the moment. I closed my eyes.

"I am going to give you another shot now, Bill. Just enough to keep you conscious while we finish up here."

I watched as he pushed the syringe into my vein. I thought for a moment that he hadn't used an alcohol wipe and mightn't that cause an infection. Then the flash of my death just moments away brought a tear to my eye, and the realization that the infection should be the least of my worries right now. I felt the now familiar warmth spreading through me. I could watch as Father Daniels walked around me hooking long ropes to the arms of the cross I was on.

I saw him pull another long cord and the ropes pulled tight. Then the cross was moving, rising and turning to stand me upright like the others. Father Daniels guided the cross so that it fell onto, or into a base of some sort. I was vertical and pain was pummeling me from all sides. Both hands felt like the spikes were ripping them in two. My ankles swelled with an increasing pain. More and more pressure as if more weight was added each second. I turned my eyes skyward and screamed.

"God can't help you now, Bill." Father Daniels was actually smiling.

He climbed up on a small stool or chair and unhooked the ropes from either arm of the cross. He leaned against the side and I moved. The base was on wheels. He turned me and moved me alongside the last living crucified form. The smell was almost as overpowering as the pain. Father Daniels stood back. He was admiring his work.

Father Daniels approached and pulled something from his pocket. He unfolded it and I saw that it was a knife. He reached up. Fear made me squirm, wide eyed, even though each slight movement sent murderous pain through my body. He used the knife to remove my underwear, I was naked. Naked, and crucified. *How long can I last without food and water? Two, maybe three days?*

"Bill, are there any last words you would want me to hear?"

I looked down at him with hatred and fear.

"I guess not." He moved forward. "For your sins, of a sexual nature against the young women of our community, you are sentenced to die." He reached up and I felt him tugging at my privates. The knife came up and with a few quick strokes his hands fell away. A second later my groin became the center of all pain. A white-hot fire was burning where my cock and balls used to be. Looking down I could see them resting in Fathers Daniels' hand. I could feel the blood running down both of my legs, a hot, fast running fluid. With a flick of his wrist, I watched as he tossed my parts down to slap against the base I was mounted on. He used the remnants of my underwear to wipe the blade clean and then tossed them to the floor near the base.

This isn't happening. Dear God, let me wake up. My mind was rupturing with the shock and horror of what I was witnessing. He couldn't have removed my penis that easily, could he? It's got to be some sort of joke, a slight of hand, right? I was getting dizzy. The pain and emotional torture was becoming too much. The loss of blood was just making things worse.

"Bill? It looks likes you are going to bleed out really quickly. Would you like me to sit with you as you go?"

My mind was whirling. I knew I was dying, I knew it was coming soon. This bastard was standing there watching me die and enjoying it. *Do I want you to sit with me? Mother fucker, you're the reason I'm dying. You're killing me, you shit for brains.* Without knowing why, I said, "Yes."

I was in so much pain. Pain like nothing I thought possible before today. Up and down were constantly changing places. I was getting nauseous and threw up. Bile and small bits of food dribbled down my chin. I watched as Father Daniels, now so much larger than life, pulled a chair over and sat down. He was looking up at me with wonder in his eyes. He reached into his jacket and pulled out a small flask from which he took a sip. He didn't offer me any. When I again opened my eyes, Father Daniels was sitting there smiling. He had a contented, peaceful look, like he was pleased with the outcome. His eyes never left my face.

A bright light. Heaven? Hell? I could sense my body giving out. I was breathing very shallow and my heart rate was weak and erratic. It didn't seem long enough. I shouldn't die this quickly.

A sudden shift and I was looking at myself hanging on the cross, the bloody spikes tearing my flesh, my naked form, pale and lifeless, my groin a mess of pulped skin and veins. I was dead. I was thinking.......

*   *   *   *

"Father...Father Daniels."

It was Detective Matthews. Father Daniels waved him over and stepped away from the three older ladies to whom he was giving his undivided attention. They smiled and moved on.

"Detective Matthews. It has been a while. I am still so shocked about Bill Thompson. Any word yet?"

"That's why I'm here Father. We found him."

"Dead?"

"Yes, Father. A bloody mess too. His hands and feet were mutilated and his cock, oh excuse me, Father, his privates had been removed."

"Removed, oh dear. Do you think he suffered?"

"Not much, Father. These wounds would have bled him out quickly. Maybe a few minutes." The detective looked like he wanted to add more.

"What is it, detective?"

"Well, Father. This is the fourth body we have found in the last six months with similar mutilations. We think we have a serial killer hanging around. Would you tell us if you have ever heard anything like that?"

"Ummm. I wouldn't want to break the sanctity of the confessional or of this office as I stated the last time we spoke, but if I really thought there was someone like that I was dealing with, I think I would find a way to help stop him."

"Thank you, Father. Do you still have my card?"

"Yes, in my office. I will use it if I hear anything."

"That's all I can ask, Father. Sorry to have to tell you about Bill like that. Oh, and sorry for the language."

"No problem, detective. I hear all sorts of words in my profession. There is little that shocks me today. Is that advancement?" He shrugged his shoulders for emphasis. "Not for me to say."

"Well, goodbye, Father."

"Bless you, Detective, in life and in work."

The detective nodded and walked towards the front of the church and out the door into the sunlight. Father Daniels made his way to the confessional. After an hour, bored out of his head by hearing little old ladies confess their savage thoughts and apologies for using the Lord's name in vain, Father Daniels finally smiled.

"Bless me, Father, for I have sinned. It has been two months since my last confession."

Father Daniels recognized the voice. He also knew what was coming and waited anxiously.

"Father, I did it again. I just got out of jail from doing it…what, three months ago."

"Doing what my son?"

"Beating the shit out of my girlfriend. I don't want to do it. She makes me."

Father Daniels nodded knowingly and held back a smile as he listened and planned the night's festivities.

THE END

The Goodbye Tear

I walked up the driveway and entered the house. When I closed the door behind me, I could tell immediately that the house was empty. It just had that feel. It didn't smell right either. It smelled of medicine and death, sweat and urine, and decay. I couldn't believe that I was here, that this had happened, that it was over, that I had missed saying goodbye. I was standing silently in the living room. There in the far-left corner was her favorite chair, with a quilted blanket lying over it. The armrests were threadbare where her hands had rubbed it these many years. A small metal TV dinner table sat just to its right and was piled high with medicine bottles, a tissue box, two or three 'Reader's Digests', and a paper folded to the crossword. Things hadn't changed much. This is how I remembered it from when I left here twenty-three years ago.

In the corner like the big, failing black piece of shit that it was, was the baby grand piano that no one has played since uncle Eddie died almost twenty-five years ago. Now it just sat there holding up what appeared to be about four hundred pounds of old dusty pictures and frames. I walked over to look at the display. Half of the pictures were in black and white and very faded. The others were in early Kodacolor. Hell, I don't think they've made that stuff since the late '70s. The images leaching and breaking apart underneath the cheap glass boundary that struggled to keep it all together. The latest picture of me looked like it was taken when I was still in high school. I'm forty-one now. I guess I wasn't around that much. I picked up one of the pictures to look at it. It must have been taken at one of our famous family get-togethers like on the Fourth of July or on Labor Day. Smiling people were in the background, most were carrying cans of beer. Boy, I could sure use one of those right now.

There were a few more recent photos of my sister and brother. They had stayed here, to stay close to the person who was carrying their weight too. They were always asking Mom for money for this and that. It made me mad that they took advantage of the one person doing them any good at all. Staying here would have smothered me, so I had chosen to leave. The day after I had graduated high school I was being sworn into the Marines. Hoo-rah!

I glanced around and was upset by what I saw. I should have been here. I should have done more. This was about my mother. This room need painting and I shuddered to think what some of the other rooms looked like. What the hell were Jerry and Joanne doing? They must have seen what was happening. They were just too fucking lazy to do anything about it since it didn't affect them. And Joanne's husband, Bill or Bob, or whatever, was a piece of work too. He and I had some unfinished business I was hoping to take care of before the day was over.

I shook my head, ashamed of them, and of me, and headed to the kitchen. I opened the fridge and dug to the back to find the beer that I knew was in there. I twisted off the top and drained half of the beer quickly. The smells in here weren't much better, not at all like I remembered. I thought they would never get that sauce smell out of these walls. I was wrong. I closed my eyes again and shook my head.

*　　　　*　　　　*　　　　*

I had just gotten off of the bus and ran the two blocks home. I ran up the stoop and flung open the door which hit the wall behind it with a loud thud. "Hey, take it easy," yelled my mother's voice from the kitchen. The smells came from the kitchen too. I stood still, closed my eyes and breathed deeply. Tonight, we were having chicken cutlet parmigiana. I could tell. The house always smelled of sauce, as any good Italian's house should. Or so I've been told all my life. My nose could now tell the difference between spaghetti and meatballs, chicken parm, veal, sausage and lasagna. When the windows were open, I would know what was for dinner by the time I turned into the driveway. There was always a little saucer off to the side for us to take a taste from. By us, I meant me, my older brother and my younger sister. When we got home from school, we all headed to the kitchen for a plate. We were never disappointed. A little sauce, maybe a meatball and a few noodles, but always some bread, cut diagonally across the loaf. I still always cut mine like that.

*　　　　*　　　　*　　　　*

"Hey, come on, Tony."

I opened my eyes, drained the rest of the beer and set the bottle down next to its cap. I turned and saw Jerry standing there.

"I knew I would find you here," Jerry said.

"I just had to come here on the way. I can't believe the shape this house is in. Couldn't one of you do something, or ask for help to fix it up?" I was leaning on the counter thinking about all the things Mom had done for them and yet they sat by and let her home turn to shit in front of their eyes.

"She liked it like this, Tony," Jerry said.

"No one likes living in shit. You should have called me."

"Would you have come?"

"For Mom, yeah."

I walked past him back into the living room. I was supposed to meet him at his house. They were having a family dinner, and believe it or not, I was invited.

"Just give me a few minutes. I'll join you outside. Okay?"

"Sure," Jerry answered as he walked out the door.

There were plenty of memories in this house. A lot of ghosts too. Jerry looked shaken up like he'd been crying or something. Joanne had been sobbing on the phone when she gave me the news. Me. I haven't shed a tear yet and I don't know why.

*   *   *   *

Jerry's wife was nice enough. The food was pretty good. Not as good as Moms, or my own for that matter, but edible. I did notice that the bread was not cut right. Jerry should know better. Their two kids and Joanne's three were sitting in the other room, eating at the 'kids' table. I ate and drank the wine they were serving, wishing it was a beer or scotch. I would have to pick some up on the way back to the hotel. They talked about things that meant nothing to me and I sat there thinking that I was wasting my time. Their lives and mine had gone their separate ways long ago. I loved them because they were family and would do anything to protect them, but we had nothing in common anymore. Especially now that Mom was gone.

After we ate, and while the women were cleaning up the kitchen, I stepped out onto the back deck to have a cigarette. Bill, or Bob, or whichever, must have seen me out there and decided to come out too. He tried to engage me in conversation, but I cut him off right away.

"Listen," I said holding up my hand to stop him from saying anything else, "Joanne is my sister. If I ever hear about you putting a hand on her again, or on the kids, they're going to find your body parts spread across the tri-state area."

"Oh, so you think you're a tough guy?" he said stepping real close into my personal space. He was trying to intimidate me because he was a little taller. It didn't work.

I slapped him hard with my left hand and when his head snapped back to the front my fist brushed his nose and I held it there. He hadn't even moved yet.

"Don't touch my sister. Got it?"

His eyes were burning. He didn't like being touched.

"Don't like it much, do ya?"

He hated losing. "Yeah, yeah." He turned and walked away. I'm pretty sure I heard him mutter 'ass hole' under his breath before he closed the door again.

When I finally went back inside, Jerry and Joanne wanted to talk about the house and about Mom's estate. I wanted none of it. They could have whatever they wanted and sell the rest. Give it to charity. Joanne was crying again, holding a bunched-up tissue just like Mom, and her mother had done before her. It must be genetic. I told them to separate it the way they wanted to. They had their kids' futures to think about. I was alone and had things under control. Joanne insisted that she would get my share to me when all was settled. I consented just to shut her up.

*   *   *   *

I walked up to the church. I hadn't been here since I left high school. I saw people lined up to say things to me about my mom. Some of the people I recognized, faces from the distant past, the rest were strangers to me. I shook their hands and listened but heard nothing. I sat in the front pew and glanced around at the surroundings. I was pretty sure that the pews were new, or at least refinished and rearranged. There was a new paint scheme too. When I was here, the walls and columns were all painted the same off white. I remember because Mom had 'volunteered' me one summer, when I was fifteen, I think, to help renovate it over my summer vacation. What a way for a kid to spend his summer. Now, it was white and a pastel blue. The stained-glass windows all looked the same, but the 'Stations of the Cross' were all new. They were now like 3D paintings or something. Not at all like the ancient paintings that I remembered.

The organist was warming up and people were milling around, and I was trying to get this headache to go away. I closed my eyes for a moment.

*   *   *   *

"I'm so proud of you, Anthony."

She always called me Anthony. Dad and everyone else called me Tony, but Mom always called me Anthony. I looked down to find her straightening my tie.

"Why, Mom?"

"You are getting confirmed today, Anthony. It is very important. Today you are becoming a man in God's eye. Anything that you do from this day forward, good or bad, he will know about it and keep it on his list. Today the slate is being washed clean. A new start for you."

"Oh, Ma, you know I'm always good," I said.

Mom laughed. "Of course, you are, Anthony. You look real nice in this suit too."

"Yeah? Like a made guy, huh?"

"Oh, stop that. We're not Mafia. No one in this family is."

"Hey, Tony."

I looked up to see Sal trotting over. We were going to sneak out and have a cigarette before things got started.

"I gotta go Ma."

"I see how good a job you guys did in here. It looks beautiful. Father Thomas told me how good you had been for him. We're proud of you, Anthony."

"Oh, Ma," I said as I turned and ran off with Sal.

*   *   *   *

"Tony, you have to stand." The voice and tap on the shoulder brought me back to the present.

I opened my eyes to see the priest, Joanne and Jerry leading the coffin down the aisle. She was crying again. I still hadn't. The priest talked, "blah-blah-blah…amen." A muffled "amen" came from the congregation. Sit, stand, sing and kneel. Up and down at seemingly random points in time. Hell, this wasn't a church service, it was like doing one of those Jane Fonda workout videos. The sermon was okay. The priest said a few nice things about Mom. Some lady, apparently a friend of Moms, got up and said a few nice things too. When Joanne got up to say something, after the first few words, she broke down and had to be led off the podium. No one asked if there was anything I wanted to say. I guess they all knew how I felt about Mom and them all ready.

The priest led the procession down the main aisle and out through the front doors. He was followed by the coffin, then the family and finally the friends. I stayed seated and left last. I'm not sure why. I looked up at the large crucifix on the wall behind the altar. I was sort of amazed by the brutality shown there, which was very realistic. The bleeding on the face from the thorn crown looked real and I bet that if you could put your hand into the wound on Christ's side that it would come out wet. I stood up and while turning away said, "Take good care of her." I walked out into the bright light as the others watched the coffin being closed into the back of the hearse.

Jerry, Joanne and a lot of the people watching were crying or hanging their heads. I took it all in still wondering why I hadn't cried yet. Mother was gone. Didn't that mean something? It meant everything. So why hadn't I cried? I didn't have an answer, and that pissed me off, a little.

*   *   *   *

Joanne had set it up for everyone to go back to her house on the way to the cemetery. Apparently, there was a scheduling difference of a few hours, and being Italian, that meant they had to eat. There were probably fifty people crammed into Joanne's house. She had a nice food spread laid out. There was ziti, a ham, a stack of sandwiches from the local deli, and of course wine, beer, liquor, soda for the kids and coffee. I ate a plate of what I could grab on the one pass through the kitchen. The rest of the time I sipped on some scotch between my beers. People were talking about the past. What Mom had done for them, telling anecdotes, some of which I am sure weren't totally truthful, but got a laugh anyway from the listeners.

I guess everyone could tell that I wasn't in the mood to talk and they left me pretty much alone in my thoughts. How could three children, raised in the same house, by the same parents, be so different? I had spent twelve years in the Marines and have travelled two or three times around the world. I had fought in many places, some of which have no names. Didn't then, don't now. I had been in countries that don't exist anymore. Helped a few of them change leaders too, but I'm not supposed to talk about that. Now, I run a private security firm on the west coast for high dollar execs and their families. Money wasn't an issue.

Jerry was a salesman at a local electronics wholesale company. He was middle management and that was as far as he would ever go. His wife knew it and had accepted it. They lived comfortably in a decent neighborhood and still managed, with the two kids, to take family vacations every few years. He had never been in trouble or in a fight. He wouldn't know what to do if he did. He would probably call me to get him out of it I guess.

Joanne was a nurse. She worked hard at work and at home. Her husband, Bill or Bob, or whichever, worked in a factory a few miles away running the production floor. Or something like that. I didn't care. I would be back if he touched her again and part of me wished he would. I didn't like him and would enjoy the humiliation of what I would do to him. Okay, I wouldn't kill and dismember him like I had told him, but he didn't know that. They were better off than Jerry, but not by much.

Two middle class families, from a middle-class family still all living in the same town. How American. How quaint. I guess my life had jaded me to the simpler things like that. They seemed happy enough. I did wonder why, if they were doing so well, they were still sponging off of their mother. Mother let them. She knew what she was doing. Knew where she was needed. She also spoiled the crap out of her grandchildren. That too ran in the family.

*　　　　*　　　　*　　　　*

"Anthony. Get the door for your grandmother."

I ran to the door and helped the aging woman into the house. I loved my grandmother. We all did. Every visit meant new and exciting tales and presents, lots of presents. Grandfather had travelled a lot and took grandmother with him. She would tell us all about foreign cities, exotic foods and delights. She would bring some of those things for us to try too. We were spoiled and didn't mind it at all. I cried a lot when my grandparents died. They were killed in a plane accident in the southern part of France.

I could still see her smiling face when I closed my eyes. She loved us, each in her own way. She told me once that she would never worry about me. That she knew I could take care of myself and that I would watch over the others. I was just a kid and never paid attention until she was gone. She knew me. I made it a point that whenever I had been stationed near a location of one of her tales, I would visit it and toast them both. I did a lot of drinking. I hoped I had made her proud. Not with the drinking, but with my life and by remembering.

*   *   *   *

"You coming?" Joanne was standing in front of me. There was no one else in the house. "We have to leave now to get to the cemetery in time."

I nodded and got up.

"You were really out of it there, Tony. You feeling all right?"

"Yes, Sis, just a little tired I guess. Jet lag maybe."

She led me out of the house. I took my rental car and followed hers down the street. We had a thirty-minute ride in front of us. I turned on the radio and started flipping through the channels to find something to listen to. The world was conspiring. The first eight or nine stations that came in were having commercials, so I moved on. The first one with music filled the car with one of Mom's favorite Neil Diamond songs. I turned it up and remembered. Remembered hearing Mom singing it loudly, and poorly I must add, while she did the housework on Saturday mornings. She drove us all crazy.

I could picture her, with those huge curlers in her hair, pushing the vacuum and belting out this song. Or maybe she would be standing over the large basket of clothes that were waiting to be ironed and she would stop to sing it. She loved this song. As much as I hated the song, I loved my mother.

The casket had been placed over the hole and was draped with silk and flowers. There were chairs for the family on one side and plenty of people standing all around it. The same priest as earlier spoke about dust and earth and souls. Did they ever talk about anything else? Finally, it was over. People walked away holding hands. Joanne was being held up by her husband. I caught his eye and found no love for me in it. The kids understood what was going on. Some were crying. Others, like me, weren't.

All the cars left but mine. I sat there and waited. About twenty minutes after the service, a grounds truck pulled up and three large men climbed out. They folded the silk and placed the large baskets of flowers into the back of the truck. They then took a hold of thick wide ropes and I watched as they lowered the casket out of sight. They pulled the ropes out, rolled them up and tossed them into the truck. Then the lowering apparatus came apart to join the rope in the truck.

Out came the shovels, and the dirt, which had been hidden from view under a green tarp, quickly disappeared into the hole. They knew what they were doing. I closed my eyes for a moment to help shake this headache.

*   *   *   *

I was sweating and covered with dirt. I had planted six of the seventeen bushes Mom had picked up that morning. Jerry was helping, a little, but got in the way more then he helped. He was just coming back carrying two glasses of lemonade and Mom was standing on the back stoop calling to me.

"Make sure you keep them in a straight line, Anthony."

"Yes, Mom."

"I want them evenly spaced too, Anthony."

"Yes, Mom."

"Not too deep either, they have to breathe."

"Yes, Mom."

"Don't you 'yes, Mom' me, Anthony."

I smiled and raised the cold glass in thanks. She smiled and went back inside. When I had started the planting that morning, it had taken a long time to fill the holes back in. It seemed to me that it had taken a long time for me to get the hang of how to use the shovel efficiently. I was losing half of the dirt each time, and working way too hard to fill in around the bushes. Jerry would balance the plant while I packed the dirt in around their roots. By this sixth one, I had it down to a science. I knew how to stand and how to swing the shovel to get the most out of it. Once you figured out a technique, it became easy.

*   *   *   *

I opened my eyes. They had a similar technique. They had been doing this a long time. When they were finished, they placed the head stone onto the waiting stand. Then, they were done. They drove off. I climbed out and walked over to the grave to read the stone. Her name had been added to Dad's head stone. Now both names, birthdates and death dates appeared.

I drove out of the main gate and headed back towards Joanne's house. I had to say goodbye. The headache was still bothering me and now my eyes were starting to get blurry. I was getting hot, flushing. I hoped that I wasn't catching something, and I pulled over to the side of the road. I felt my head and knew I wasn't feverish. My eyes were still burning, and I felt a pressure in my chest. Was I having a heart attack? I looked into the rear-view mirror to see my face. As I did so, a solitary tear slid down my cheek. That's what I was feeling. My heart had broken. I finally cried for my mother. I closed my eyes again and said "Goodbye, Mom."

THE END

Killer

Have you ever had one of those days? Mine went like this…

I woke up late because the alarm clock battery had died during the night. I got into the shower to find out that there was no hot water. I hit every fucking traffic light on the way to work. I spilled my cup of coffee all over my lap when I reached for the phone. That call was an invitation to a meeting that was happening right now! My pen ran out of ink as I was writing down the follow-up tasks assigned to me. At lunch time, to save time, I hit a fast food drive-through. When I got back to my desk, I found out that I didn't get what I had ordered. I worked hard all afternoon trying to finish up a hundred-page report when my computer froze up two hours in. The IT guy came and when he finally got it working, he informed me that all my work was lost. I sat back closed my eyes and decided that I couldn't wait to get home and crawl into bed. What could happen there, right? Right?

*   *   *   *

Out of breath, I lay down beside the woman. I was dizzy from the assertion and my heart was thundering behind my ribs. I was sweaty and sticky and very spent. I could feel some warm liquid dripping onto my stomach and wiped it across my chest with my left hand. My right hand was still trapped under the woman's shoulder. I closed my eyes and saw her still beneath me wriggling. Trying desperately to get away from me as the knife was pushed deep into her stomach, and then between her ribs, again and again.

I pulled out of her and shifted my body over hers to push myself deep into one of the new holes in her abdomen. The blood was running freely from the wounds as I shoved myself into her over and over. Loud sucking sounds accompanied each thrust in and out of her. The climax was getting closer with each knife penetration. My orgasm finally coming moments after the light in her eyes went out.

I looked at myself in the mirror that was mounted from the ceiling. Both of our bodies were wet with her blood which looked so dark in the candlelight. It was darker still against our winter-whitened skin. I watched as my chest pumped up and down rapidly trying to get air into it, the action slowing down as time went by and I relaxed. Hers had remained unmoving. Without knowing why, I dipped my index finger into the blood and tasted it. It was a little salty, maybe with a metallic hint, but also sort of sweet.

After a few minutes, I stood up and made my way to the shower. The hot water cascaded over me turning red by the time it hit the drain. Standing under the hot waterfall relaxing, I watched as the rinsing water finally cleared. I stayed like that for a long time hoping that the water could clean more than my skin. I toweled off and slipped my underwear back on. I dressed while looking over at the body in the bed. It was cooling off and still draining, small rivulets of blood snaking across her smooth skin and pooling under her. Her eyes were fully glazed now, and her beauty was leaving her quickly, never again willing to grace my vision.

The whole drive home I thought about her. I thought about her passion, her smile and her blood. I could still taste it in my mouth when I ran my tongue over my teeth. I made it home later than I had hoped and tossed my clothes over onto the floor and climbed into bed wearing just my underwear. I pulled the sheet up close to my chin and snuggled down in its warmth. Funny, I was having trouble remembering the woman's name. In moments I was asleep having been so tired by the evening's business.

I have dreams like that a lot. Dreams where things are going along just right, and then, whammo. I'm holding a knife or a gun and doing things with them I could never do in real life, when I was awake. Why do I have these dreams? Is it because I do not do them when awake? Couldn't do them when awake?

I awoke.

Today was different. I could sense it. I got out of bed and went through my morning ritual. I brushed my teeth, took a quick shower, and then brushed my hair. I pulled some clothes out of the dresser and placed them on the bed. I flipped on the television to catch the news while I pulled myself together. When I was dressed, I picked up the discarded clothes from the floor to get my wallet, keys and the assorted other pocket-carried items. I was emptying those pockets when I saw it. On the cuff of one of my pants legs there was dried blood, a lot of it. No, that couldn't be blood, right? It had to be mud or something I stepped in last night. I lifted the leg and looked closer. No, it was blood. How the hell did that get there?

I was trying to figure it out, when the news mentioned a murder last night. I glanced over at the television and lost my breath. There on the screen was a picture of my dream-girl from last night. They were talking about how she was found this morning all cut up and dead in her apartment. No way. I had dreamt all of that, hadn't I? The news about the murder had lasted about a minute, but then I started flipping between the other stations trying to gather more information. It was true. It was happening again.

I walked to the bathroom and checked myself in the mirror. I looked the same. I had showered, but I quickly removed my clothes and started examining my body. I found a few scratches. *Oh, shit.* I also found what could be dried blood under one of my fingernails. *Oh, shit.*

*　　　　*　　　　*　　　　*

The traffic today sucked. It was a back to school day which meant that every mother was back on the road clogging it up on their way to that super sale at one of those new large we've-got-everything stores. Busses were stopping at every damned corner. Kids were strolling across the street in groups, flashing their fingers in defiance at those who honked to hurry them up. And don't forget the school crossing guard that stopped the traffic five minutes before each kid got to the corner, and then waited until the kids were almost in the school to release the line of cars idling to get on with their lives. The old bastard.

Work was rough today. Meeting after meeting, with little time between to catch up on the things they wanted from you from the last one. Hell, they didn't need me in most of them. I sat there quietly listening, trying oh so hard not to fall asleep. I sipped on my coffee and played with my pen. I occasionally took notes when I didn't have to, just to look like I was doing something, like paying attention. Really, I was sitting there thinking about that woman. The memories had come back to me. I could see her face, feel her body and taste her blood. I was so glad that I didn't have to stand up at this meeting because I was so hard under my pants and knew that it would show.

I stopped for a few beers and a steak on the way home. The restaurant was full and my waitress, Carla, paid little attention to my needs. She had nice legs and a nice smile, which I bet got her the job. As I ate, I knew that she and I would meet later. She would take care of my needs then. I smiled and licked my fingers. I left her a nice tip and headed home. I took a shower and lay on the bed watching television. There was nothing on again, so I continually flipped around the channels. As I started nodding off, I set the shut-off timer for thirty minutes and shut my eyes.

*　　　　　*　　　　　*　　　　　*

My needs had definitely been met. Carla had done everything she could think of to keep alive. I think half of the local hookers would have been shocked by her performance. The hardest thing I had to deal with was keeping her nasal passages open so that she wouldn't suffocate before I wanted her to. The gag had kept her crying and screaming to a minimum, but it got in the way from time to time. She had had two cats which didn't last too long. She watched as I took each one in turn and sat there petting them. Then I suddenly snapped their necks. I left them lying on the bed next to her head, as a reminder.

I've learned over the years how to use the knife to inflict pain and bleeding, without killing right away. How deep I can push a knife into the abdomen, where the arm and leg major arteries are and how not to hit them. Pressing a knife in between the ribs is very painful, but if you collapse a lung, the fun is over too quickly. What's the old adage, practice, practice, practice? Carla was losing blood at an alarming rate at this point, twenty minutes into the night. We have had sex five or six different ways, and I am disappointed and tell her so.

I leaned across her and grabbed the two pillows stacked by the headboard. I lifted her by the waist with one hand and wedged the pillows under her, raising her ass up off of the bed. I sucked on my finger and then pressed it slowly and steadily into her ass. She squirmed some, but I don't think she thought it was too bad. Better than the knife, I guess. I pulled out my finger and walked away from her, into her bathroom.

I opened cabinets and drawers until I found the Vaseline. I spread it liberally around her hole and up and down my forearm. I slowly pushed my hand into her. Her body spasmed and her eyes were filled with panic. I opened and closed my fingers to feel her insides. She was bucking against her restraints and looking at me with terror. I pulled my hand out holding a section of her intestine. I pulled out a small knife and cut through the snake-shaped mess in my hands. I then pushed the short end back inside before I started pulling the rest of them out of her natural hole to show her. I played with them like a feather boa and wrapped them around my neck and tossed them from hand to hand. Carla's eyes grow large and she squirmed and bounced on the bed. It took a few minutes before the majority of her was out and lying on the bed. I let her see them, and then I started placing them in rings across her now shallow belly.

Damn, she had passed out. I spent a few more minutes playing with her body, before climaxing onto the bed. I decided to rearrange her position and to tie the two cats to her with her intestines. *There, I was finished.* I made my way to her shower and spent a long time enjoying the pulsing hot water as it relaxed and revived my tiredness. While getting dressed I wondered what had possessed me to remove her insides. I think it just came down to, *why not.* I took a last look around the room and smiled down at my work. So nice to have something that goes my way once in a while. Life is hard sometimes and boy does this help.

*   *   *   *

The alarm woke me, and I shut it off. I'm not one of those hit the snooze button four or five times kinda guys. I ran a hand across my face trying to wake up. I got a whiff of shit and looked down at my hand. I didn't see anything and looked at the bed around me. Nothing there either. Then it hit me, and I remembered the girl from last night, the disemboweling and re-positioning. I guess the shit smell didn't come off in the shower. I sat up in bed, turned on the television and switched to the news. There was nothing at all about the girl.

I got up and made breakfast, coffee and toast, the kind with raisins and cinnamon in it. The morning news had nothing of significance in it today. Gas is up, oil is up, and stocks are down. *No shit,* I think, while downing the last of the coffee. I placed the cup in the sink and headed to the shower. While cleaning off, I decided to stop by the store on the way home today to get of those pulsing shower heads. It had felt so good last night at that girl's apartment.

Work sucked today, as usual. It seemed that everything I touched turned to shit. I had to re-do every report at least twice. Murphy must have been sitting on the edge of my desk all afternoon laughing his ass off. I sent a report by email and it came back as undeliverable. Just what the hell does that mean? I checked the report, saved it again, zipped it to shrink the size of the file and tried sending it again. I sat there almost twenty minutes waiting for that fucking hourglass thing to go away telling me that the report went through. Thankfully it got there in time, barely.

I got an email from my boss at about two-thirty, busting my ass about something that went wrong. I had no idea what the fuck he was talking about. After a few calls, wasting my time, it turns out that he had meant to send his ire to someone else. Lucky me, I had to point out one of his errors to an already pissed-off boss.

I could really use a diversion tonight, I thought as I sat there trying to close out the day on an upturn. I closed my eyes for a moment and thought about the girl from last night. I remembered the feelings so intensely that I got a little giddy and hard. I opened my eyes to find my hand rubbing my engorged crotch under the desk. Thankfully no one had noticed. I glanced around and sat back and picked up my cold coffee. It tasted like crap now, but it took my mind off of the other thing.

On the way home from work, I did stop by the home store and got myself one of those multiple nozzle pulsating showerheads. It took me a few minutes to hook it up after I ate dinner and I stepped into the relaxing water to check it all out. *Now, to go out hunting.* I dried off and dressed for the occasion in dark jeans and pull over shirt. I finished by tying my black sneakers in a double knot so that I wouldn't have to worry about them coming undone and maybe losing one. As I was finishing, my story came on the news. The girl's neighbor had looked in on her and found her. It was so horrible.

A smile came to my face as the anchor woman told of how the police were looking for witnesses, anyone that might have seen a man leaving or entering the apartment. None of her neighbors had heard anything, which puzzled the police because of the manner in which she was brutally attacked. More on the story tonight at eleven, they said, and I laughed. Tonight, by eleven they just might have much more to report on.

*　　　　*　　　　*　　　　*

The hardware store had just the right things that I wanted. I picked out a good hatchet, a Bowie style hunting knife and a self-lighting torch for soldering. I also bought some piping and solder so that the purchase wouldn't raise any suspicion. I placed the items in a small gym bag that I kept in the car and headed a few miles east of where I lived to look in a nicer part of town. I drove with the windows down, letting the cool evening air keep me alert. There she was. I noticed a woman jogger and drove to a corner to watch where she went.

I had gotten lucky. I followed the woman for about a mile. She finally turned into the driveway of an older house. There was only one car in the driveway, a beat-up, ten-year-old, mid-sized sedan. I waited until she was inside for a few minutes before walking up to look inside of the car. Good. There was no child-seat or toys on any of the seats. What I did see was a lot of drive-up coffee cups and wrappers. She was jogging to keep the weight off her ass after eating all that shit every day. It also meant that she lived alone and that we probably wouldn't be interrupted.

I drove my car two blocks away and walked back to the house. I was carrying the gym bag and I was sure that no one, if they noticed, would think it strange. As soon as I got there, I knocked on the front door. No answer. I knocked again. This time I heard, 'coming' from inside. The woman came to the door. As soon as the door-opening was wide enough, I punched her hard in the face. I heard a crack and she staggered back and fell onto the hardwood floor. I quickly closed the door behind me and locked it.

I pulled her by her arm, sliding her along the floor down a long hallway until I found her room. Her other hand was covering her bleeding nose and she was crying. I helped lift her up, to sit on the edge of the bed. She looked at me without asking the obvious questions. I just smiled and punched her again. She collapsed on the bed, unconscious. I got to work.

When the woman opened her eyes again, she found that she was sitting in her desk chair, nude and gagged. I had used duct tape to secure her. Her feet were bent under the chair and taped to the wheel support beams. Her head was whipping around, apparently looking for something. When she looked at me, I could see her body sort of fold in on itself. She knew then that it was over for her. She knew instinctively what was going to happen over the next few hours.

I took out the hatchet and showed it to her. Her eyes grew large and her chest rose and fell in a fast, panicked state. I took her left hand in mine, bent down to kiss the back of it and stood up. I swung the hatchet at the wrist. It took three chops to sever the hand. I picked it up and kissed the back of it again. The woman was bouncing the chair all around the room, her damaged wrist pumping blood across the floor, making it slick. I pulled the chair back and picked the torch up out of the gym bag. I lit it and showed it to her. I then used it to cauterize the wound, closing the arteries and veins in the wrist, to help keep her alive longer. She passed out from the pain, or maybe the sight of her burning flesh.

I went to her bathroom and washed the blood from my hands and to grab a towel to get some of it off of the floor. I didn't want to be slipping all over the place and falling. When the woman opened her eyes, she found me using her severed hand to stimulate her sexually. Her eyes flashed at me with terror and hate. I kissed her forehead. I was naked and aroused, which I think upset her. Over the next hour and a half, the hatchet and knife became bloodier. I could have gone on all night, but her heart had given out. Apparently, she had lost too much blood to keep the remaining parts of her alive.

I showered and cleaned my blades. I put my clothes back on, placed all of my tools back in the bag and put the bag near the front door so that I couldn't forget it when I left. I spent a few minutes placing the woman's parts on the bed in the correct order. First her upper arm, then her lower arm and finally her hand. I did that with both arms, except that I decided at the last moment to leave her left hand inside of her, where I felt she would want it. I took in the view and thought that I had done well. I made my way to her kitchen and found a soda in the refrigerator to quench my thirst.

I sat in her living room and watched the evening news. I must have fallen asleep. I woke up to find myself still in her house with the sun up. I looked at my watch and saw that it was after eight in the morning. I was late for work. *Oh, well.* I picked up my bag and walked out of her front door, leaving it open behind me.

*   *   *   *

I walked into Doctor Newman's office.

"Stacie, please call…"

"Hi, Jim, I didn't think you had an appointment today."

"Shut up…call 911 and then leave. Oh, and take them with you." I pointed to the two patients sitting in the waiting room.

"Jim, what are you talking about? Hey, is that blood on your hand?"

I looked down. "Yes, but don't worry, it's not mine. Now do what I told you." I started for the inner office door. "Do it. Now!"

I opened the door to Doctor Newman's office. He looked up at me. "I'm with someone, Jim. You're going to have to wait."

I turned to the patient and said, "Get the hell out." They got up and left. The look on my face must have let them know that I was serious.

"Jim, you can't be doing this. There are protocols to follow…"

He stopped when he saw the three drivers' licenses, I tossed onto his desk. The third one stuck to the paper because the blood on it wasn't quite dry yet. "Jim, what have you done?"

"It started again, Doc." I pushed the door closed and walked behind his desk. His hands were still holding the licenses over the desk. I reached and pulled his left hand away and smashed the Bowie knife down into the desk right through his hand. He let out a horrific howl. He grabbed his wrist like that was supposed to help ease the pain. "I can't go on like this, Doc. This has to end."

"Jim…we can work…something out…" he was saying between ragged breaths. "There are new…medications…"

"I don't want new meds, Doc. Don't you get it? I'm done. This is it. Game over."

Doctor Newman looked at Jim as if seeing him for the first time. "Jim, please…don't do this."

"Doc, I told Stacie to call the police and to leave. If she did, they should be here soon." I walked around the room nervously. "You did all that you could, Doc. This isn't about you. And it's not your fault. I'm the killer, the sick one."

"Jim…" he started.

"Don't!" I yelled at him, leaning over the desk, the spit flying from my mouth landing on his glasses. "I have to end this my way. You know what I mean?"

Doctor Newman did understand, and he also knew that right now he had to let this play out. If he antagonized Jim anymore, he would get hurt and maybe killed. Jim Reilly had killed six women before coming to Doctor Newman's office almost eight years ago. Doctor Newman had helped Jim turn himself in. The courts saw that Jim was sick and confined him to the state hospital where Doctor Newman saw him three times a week. After seven years, Doctor Newman and another doctor talked the court into letting Jim free. They believed that they had found the answers that Jim had been looking for. His psychosis was treated, and all indications were that he was better and there was no reason to keep him locked up. The courts agreed. That was six months ago.

Jim had been to Doctor Newman's office once a week since then with no problems. Apparently, Doctor Newman had been wrong.

"I'm sorry, Doc," I said while dropping down into one of the chairs.

"Jim, is there someone…you want me to call…for you?"

"No." I sat there waiting. I closed my eyes and remembered the women. I pictured all nine of them. I could see their faces. I could smell them. I could walk you through each scene in the minutest detail. For me it was as if each incident had happened this morning.

"Would you like to tell me about the latest one, Jim?"

I kept my eyes closed and walked Doctor Newman through the night. I heard him gasp a few times, but he knew not to interrupt me. When I was done, I opened my eyes and he was looking at me with a disappointed look that I had seen when I was younger, in the school's dean's office. I also saw and could smell the vomit that was on his desk now. I hadn't heard that. I got up and walked behind him to look out of the window. The day was bright, and the skies were clear, a nice day.

"Jim…I would still like to help you…if you would let me try."

"Sorry, Doc, it's too late, they're here." I could see the two police cars pulling up to the curb out in front of the building and the officers getting out. I could also see Stacie talking to them and pointing up at me. I knew she was really pointing up towards the office, which was on the third floor, but the impression in my mind was that she knew exactly where I was standing. One of the police officers spoke into his shoulder-mounted microphone and then they approached the building.

We both looked up at the door when we heard the outer-office door open.

"Hello, Doctor Newman?" One of the officers was calling.

Doctor Newman looked up at me and I nodded. "In here," he said.

The door opened and two police officers entered the room. One had his gun out and pointed at me. The other was holding his hands up in an open palm way indicating that I should take it easy. He was the one to speak.

"What's going on today, Jim?" Stacie must have given him my name. Good girl.

Doctor Newman started to say something, "Jim here wants to give himself up."

"Why don't we let Jim speak for himself, okay, Doctor Newman?" Doctor Newman nodded his understanding.

"Well, Officer, this is sort of a confession and last stand."

"Why don't we do this downtown then, Jim. It might be more comfortable for all of us."

I ignored his obvious play to take control of the situation. "I've killed nine women…"

"Really?" the officer wanted to know.

"You going to let me talk, or are you going to be an asshole?"

"I'm sorry, Jim. Please continue."

"I've killed nine women. Six of them, eight and nine years ago. The last three are the ones on the news for the last few days, and one last night I don't think you know about yet."

The officers looked at Doctor Newman, who nodded his head up and down indicating that I was telling the truth. I reached to the desk and picked up the licenses and tossed them to the officer. He looked at them and then pulled a notebook out of is breast pocket. He flipped through it and stopped. He read something and then looked up at me. "This is serious stuff, Jim."

"I know. That's why I came here and called you in."

"You called us?"

"Well, I had Stacie call you."

"And now what, Jim? Are you going to let us get Doctor Newman some medical attention? Are you going to come quietly with us?"

I glanced down at Doctor Newman's hand and the Bowie knife. I had forgotten about that. "Yes, call for the paramedics. We can talk while we wait for them."

When the officer reached for his shoulder mike, I lunged forward, pressed down on Doctor Newman's left wrist and pulled the knife out. I held the knife to his throat.

"Whoa, whoa," the officer called out. His hands were waving that 'let's take it easy' wave we all know.

I pulled the knife back and up so that I could plunge it into his chest with the down stroke that I knew, and hoped, would never come. A loud deafening explosion filled the room, and then another. I felt myself being thrown back against the glass window. Pain flooded my mind. The room stopped moving in real time and seemed to go into slow motion. The two officers were rushing at me while Doctor Newman lurched out of his chair to fall on the floor. My perspective twisted the room at a strange angle as the floor rushed up to meet me. *So, this is what it feels like,* I think as I die.

THE END

The Future and Past Collide

This is a fictionalized account of true events.
The names and places have been modified.

Sure, is hot today. Thank God the IHOP is air-conditioned.

"Damn it," Bob says, as the shopping cart he is pushing gets caught in a sidewalk crack. The crack had turned one of the wheels and caused him to walk right into the cart. The handle shoved something hard in his pocket right up between his ribs. Bob pulled the cart out of the crack and continued on his quest.

Got to remember to stop by Augie's Auto over on Forth later and get some of that used oil to put on these fucking wheels.

Bob wiped his forehead with his left forearm and waited for the light to change. Getting both carts across a busy street against the lights was an almost insane thing to attempt. Bob and his two carts could be seen all over town. The front cart, always in his sight, contained all of the important things in his life. His clothing, his little safe filled with old watches, rings and other precious items he would probably never have the need to use again. He also carried books and a large scrap book in the front cart. The second cart, which Bob pulled behind him, carried the cans and bottles he scrounged throughout the day. It also held the found jewelry that he would save, and scrap metal that was easy for him to move. Don't forget about the occasional TV or computer monitor, or even the vacuum that someone thought to toss out.

The money that he made from the returnable items more than paid for his daily needs and anything that remained he made sure to hide well. On Thursdays, after he dropped off his cans and bottles and scrap, Bob always went to IHOP for dinner. He figured that it was the least he could do for himself, his one splurge. By now, all of the waitresses knew Bob and treated him nicely. There was never an offending comment directed at Bob. Some of the customers might have looked at him like he didn't belong there and wished he was out of sight, *but fuck them*, he thought. He had earned this.

Bob left his carts near the eastern wall, in front of the windows of the IHOP. Vanessa was on duty today and smiled honestly at the old man as he came through the door. He looked around the room and asked for the window booth to keep an eye on his belongings. Vanessa knew what he wanted and sat him there. She also knew his order by heart, hot coffee followed by a large, unsweetened iced tea and the meatloaf special which came with mashed potatoes and string beans. She always made it a point to mention to the cook that it was for Bob so that he would get the extra gravy that he liked. Bob barely looked up when Frank Wilson walked in.

*   *   *   *

"And don't forget that on Tuesday we have the test on chapters nine through thirteen," Chief Petty Officer Childress added over the top of the many moans and groans.

"Five fucking chapters over the holiday weekend. He thinks we're robots," Frank's buddy Eric chimed in. "Damn it. What are you doing after class?"

"Well," Frank said, "I'm going to take a shower and go out for dinner. I'll study later tonight."

"Let me guess," Eric laughed, "IHOP again?"

"Yup, you're welcome to join me if you want." Frank tossed his books into his book bag and started for the door. Frank didn't really have plans for the weekend, so studying when everyone else was away would be a welcome relief.

"Nah, I'll hit the mess hall, study for a bit, then hit the clubs and grab something there. Have fun."

"Yeah, you too." Frank watched as Eric trotted off to catch up with Rich and Oscar. He glanced at the sky, noting that there was plenty of sunlight left and turned towards the barracks. After showering and changing into civilian jeans and a tee shirt, Frank climbed into his very old Toyota and drove through town to the IHOP.

Frank was in the Navy and in one of the top schools in the country. They were almost finished with this leg of the schooling. Two more months and then they hit the hard part, putting the two years of training into use. The dropout rate was high, and Frank had seen some of his buddies go down the tubes. He was carrying a decent GPA, so he wasn't worried about being asked to leave. Long hours studying the intense courses have kept him free to spend some days off on his own. The IHOP was for him a relief, not only from the mess hall, but from seeing nothing except Navy all the time.

The waitresses had come to know Frank and gave him a smile and a hello when he walked in the door. He waited for Connie to seat him, a booth towards the middle, but he still had a good view of the passing traffic through the streaky windows. After deciding what he was going to try tonight and placing his order, Frank glanced around and noticed the homeless man sitting by the window. They were facing each other, two booths apart and on opposite sides of the aisle. Frank gave him a nod, having gotten to be known as a regular. The homeless man nodded back then dropped his head back into the book he was reading.

Sitting back to enjoy the coffee and letting the food settle in his sated stomach, Frank again glanced at the homeless man trying to see what he was reading. Frank, after all, did read quite a lot, even with all the schoolwork. It was his passion. He has spent many hours sitting in the dorm recreation room with his headphones on and a good book carrying his mind far from the things he dealt with during the day. Some of the other sailors started calling him 'The Professor'. To Frank, the book looked like a school textbook, and curiosity got the better of him.

"Excuse me," Frank called to the man.

The man looked up at him, annoyed. "Yes?"

"I couldn't help noticing the textbook. May I ask what it is?"

The man closed the book to check the cover. "Theories of Quantum Mechanics," the man answered.

In his head, Frank heard the *sure it is* loud and clear, but he asked the man, "Wow, no offense, but why a book like that?"

"Well, I used to teach it," the man responded before setting the book down to refill his coffee cup. After all, the IHOP coffee was pretty good and the always full carafe stretched his limited funds.

Frank again heard the *sure you did* inside his head. He sort of knew he shouldn't judge people by the way they looked, but come on, a homeless physics teacher? "I'm taking a similar course down the street here…"

"NTC?"

"…uh yeah. Just don't see many people reading that sort of thing for fun."

"Even though I'm out of the scene doesn't mean the head doesn't work anymore."

Frank was dismissed. The man turned his attention back to the book and Frank knew that any further interruptions would be an annoyance, but he couldn't resist. "Where did you teach, sir?"

The man gave him a look that seemed to say *why don't you just leave me alone like the others?*, but he closed the book again. "I was a tenured professor at a major southern California college. Spent a lot of years trying to get little idiots to understand the importance of the things around them."

"What happened?" Frank was intrigued.

"One day on the way to work I just decided to keep driving. Threw it all away. Left my wife, the college and all it had to offer. And here I am…what…about ten years later."

"That sounds a little crazy," Frank said, but part of him believed the man.

The laugh that came out of the man startled everyone in the restaurant, "Could be."

The man got up, gathered his things and came over to Frank. "Anytime you need help with your studies, look for me. If I'm around, I'll try to help. You seem like a good kid." With that he turned, paid his bill and left.

Frank watched him as he put his book into his cart, looked both directions and apparently decided to head left towards downtown. After finishing his coffee, Frank walked to the counter to pay. Connie said. "Hey, Bob must really like you."

"Bob?"

"Yeah, Bob. You were just talking to him."

"His name is Bob?"

"Yeah, and he hates talking to strangers, so he must like you."

"Is he really a college professor like he was telling me?"

"I think so. He's very smart and some of us in the area watch out for him. We take care of him here. Give him extra stuff. We're not supposed to, but hey. It's the right thing to do."

"He comes here every night?"

"Every Thursday, hon."

Connie gave Frank his change and turned to catch her next order. Frank stood there feeling a little guilty about not paying more attention to the man and about not believing him.

*　　　　*　　　　*　　　　*

"I can't believe you aced that fucking test, man," Eric whispered to Frank, who sat beside him in class. Eric had only gotten a seventy-nine. Frank just smiled back. Frank had studied most of the weekend sitting outside at one of the picnic tables. Because of the holiday weekend, the place had been like a ghost town. He spread out his books and notes and had gone over everything he could think of that the Chief might spring on them. He sipped a lot of coffee during the day and a lot of beer at night. His sanity came from the headphones that seemed glued to the side of his head, filling the silence with music that drove his roommates crazy. They all wanted to know why the hell he listened to that crap. He didn't want to tell them that he felt the same way about the quote-unquote music that they tortured him with on a daily basis.

When the class was over, they both gathered their things and headed back to the dorm. Eric had duty tonight, so he headed right for the shower. Frank tossed his books onto his desk and started getting dressed in his civilian clothing. Eric came walking back into the room naked and toweling off. "I take it the pancakes are calling you?"

"Yup, want me to bring something back for you?" Frank offered.

"Nah, I'll order a pizza later. Ever think about banging one of them waitresses?"

"Oh, man, they're like sisters to me."

"Yeah, yeah, just don't catch anything, okay?" Eric added a wink before breaking out in laughter.

"Funny guy. This weekend we'll go over the new stuff together so that you can blow through the next test, okay?"

"Sure, as long as I still get time to go out and get laid."

"What does that mean, you need about five minutes?" Frank wanted to know.

That got them both laughing. Frank waved and left Eric to finish getting into his uniform.

*   *   *   *

Frank sat out in his car and took out his physics book. He wanted to find a complicated concept, that he understood, to sort of test Bob tonight. He debated with himself over the ethics of it, but decided that he really wanted to find out more about this homeless guy. If that meant tricking him a little, so be it. When he saw Bob from about three blocks away, he got out of the car and entered the restaurant. He asked to be seated near the window hoping to be near where Bob would sit.

This weather sucks, thought Bob as he wiped his forehead for the tenth time in about two minutes. *This humidity is better suited for the fucking ducks, then people.* Bob placed his carts near the front window of the IHOP and entered into the air-conditioned space. He stood in the entryway for a few minutes to cool down. He spotted Frank and inside thought about leaving, but the coolness softened his determination. He climbed into the booth behind Frank and then gave his usual order to Vanessa. Standing up, he nodded hello to Frank on his way to the bathroom to wash his hands.

When Frank was finished eating, he pulled his schoolbook up from the booth bench and started going over the 'hard part'. He wanted to see if Bob would offer any input, or if he would again have to approach him. Frank could hear when Bob pushed his plate aside and knew that he was done. He was counting in his head the passing of time, hoping. He got so caught up in his thoughts, that he didn't hear when Bob had gotten up and stood beside him, until he asked, "Ah, fluid dynamics, the wonderful magic of water."

Frank looked up startled, "Uh...yeah, sorry. Guess I got into the page."

"Stuff doesn't work quite like air, like they try to tell you most of the time. Close, in certain applications, but not all the time." Bob picked up the book to look at the title and author. 'Fluid Mechanics, by Robert Granger'. "Not bad for starters. Met the guy at a conference in Chicago, I think, or Detroit maybe." He placed the book back in front of Frank and started to move away.

"Man, this stuff is crazy." Frank was trying to get Bob engaged in a conversation, to draw him out. "Heat transfer into a fluid through a pipe. Laminar this, boundary that. I thought it would be simpler."

Bob sat across the table. Frank smiled inside. Bob pulled a very used pen out of his pocket, flipped over the unused paper placemat and started drawing.

His hand was flying around very quickly. Frank watched, hoping that the guy wasn't just drawing some nonsense, that this wouldn't be a waste of time, but he also needed to know. He sipped on his coffee until Bob was finished and spun the paper around. Frank was shocked by what he saw. This guy definitely was the real thing. The diagram was almost identical to the stuff they had been studying on the board at school.

Bob started adding arrows to point out specifics. He wrote in little notes to explain the different views and concepts. He did this upside down as he instructed Frank. Frank listened and soaked it up. Bob knew his stuff, all the way down to the details. Frank was slack jawed as Bob continued to go deeper into the real-life situations where this could be used. The concept was used in car radiators, heating a home, and even inside a nuclear reactor. *Shit. I feel like such an idiot,* thought Frank. *What happened that brought this man here?*

"If you get this, there is nothing on the tests you will see that you can't answer. Promise," Bob said, as he got up as to leave.

"Well, thank you, mister…" Even though Frank knew his name was Bob, he played it dumb.

"Just call me Bob. Everyone does."

"Okay, Bob. Thanks. That was very intense."

"Does that mean I passed the test?"

Frank just stared back at him.

"Come on, son. I can spot a bullshitter. You knew the subject. You were trying to see if I had told you the truth the last time. Right?"

Frank hung his head. "Yes, and I'm so sorry."

"No need, kid. I would have done the same thing." He picked up his coffee from his booth and sat down across from Frank again. "A homeless college professor? Yeah, right."

"So, tell me, who are you, really?"

"That's a long story," Bob admitted and sat back to sip from his cup.

Frank could tell that Bob didn't want to go there just yet, but he tried pushing a little. "I understand," he paused, "You don't know me, and I guess I shouldn't be asking about you either. I'm sorry."

"You don't have to sorry, Frank, is it? Just never thought anyone would want to know about me. Why would they?"

"Well, I do. There is something about you that makes me want to know. An attraction, not in a sexual way mind you, to see behind the front you put on. A good mind that is being unused."

Bob emptied his cup and reached for the carafe to refill it. Frank slid the sugar and milk a little closer to him. After fixing his coffee to suit his taste, Bob looked over at Frank and asked him, "Ever hear of the 'Hidden Camera Video Show'?"

"Sure, who hasn't?"

"Well, I was a professor, trying to teach physics, and one day this guy comes in and asks me to help him develop some gags for his show." Bob paused because Frank had a look on his face implying 'here we go again'. "Be right back." Bob popped up and headed for the door. Frank watched as he started rummaging around in one of his carts. A minute or so later, Bob came back in, carrying a bag of books.

Sitting at the table, he started going through the bag. He pulled out what looked to Frank to be an old photo album. He was right.

"Here," Bob said as he pushed the book over to Frank and pointed at the left-hand page. Sure enough, it was a picture of a younger Bob and the guy Frank recognized from television. Flipping through the next four or five pages, Bob pointed out multiple photos of the two of them at different scenes. Bob added commentary about what each prank had been. How he had helped design and set it up, as well as about the people that he met while doing it.

"So, you had it made," stated Frank. "What in the world would make you want to give it all up?"

"See, I had a wife. Oh, I loved her, and she loved me, but once the television shit started, I was away more and she didn't like that much. I don't blame her. There were pressures all around me; the college insisting that its leading professors get published once a year, the wife issues, having to deal with deadlines and manufacturers who are making the parts, and fucking some of them up, having to cut corners to meet schedules, students who didn't give a rat's ass about the class, but who wanted me to give them extra stuff to make up for their crappy grades."

He sat back and seemed to drift away. Frank let him go. Frank got up and paid the checks, both of them. He figured it was the least he could do for the man. Before he had gotten back to his seat, Bob had started in again, as if he had never stopped.

"So, this one day, you see, I kissed the wife good-bye, like normal, got in the car and headed for work. But somewhere along the way I just decided not to go. I pulled into the bank and withdrew a couple thousand dollars, filled the tank and just started driving." He sat there nodding his head, remembering.

Frank watched as a small tear made its way down Bob's cheek. Bob ignored it. He picked up his books, looked at Frank, and without a word got up and left. Frank sat there not knowing what to do. He had dredged up this guy's past with no insight on what it might do to the guy. Outside, Bob made his way to the corner with his carts, crossed the street and disappeared behind the laundromat without looking back.

Before leaving the IHOP, Frank asked for the manager. Frank gave him a hundred dollars and explained that Bob would not have to pay for his meals for a while. Frank told the manager that when the money ran out, he would add some more. The waitresses understood and said that they would take care of it for him. Vanessa gave Frank a hug with tears in her eyes as she thanked him.

The following Thursday, Frank got held up at school and had to go right on duty, so he didn't get to the IHOP. He wondered if Bob had been there. If he was all right after the conversation, they had had last week. Hopefully he didn't get too upset and do something stupid. It bothered Frank that he didn't know.

*　　　　*　　　　*　　　　*

Eric insisted that none of what the teacher had gone over was on the test. "I mean, where the hell did you read that stuff? How did you know it?" They were walking back towards the dorm. "You are such an asshole, Frank."

"Why, because I did the work and didn't try to skim through it. I told you I would have helped you last weekend, but all you did was go out. Don't blame me."

"Yeah, you're right. Sorry."

"Just read it again over the next few nights and I'll fill in the blanks, okay?"

"Sure, now you're giving me homework."

"Hey, up to you, pal, all up to you." Frank was finishing getting dressed to go out himself. He had missed going to the IHOP last week and was still worried about Bob. "See you later, got to go."

He shouldn't have worried. As he pulled up to the restaurant, he could see Bob out front leaning against his cart, waiting. He climbed out and headed to meet him.

"Hey, Bob. How you feeling?"

"You did a good thing for me son, but I wish you hadn't."

Frank didn't let down his guard. "I'm sorry, if the memories were too painful. I didn't mean for that to happen."

"Not that, the money. I do okay for myself, okay? You shouldn't have done it."

"Thought I was doing something nice for a friend, but I can stop it if you like."

"Just ask next time, okay? I'm not some charity case."

"I didn't see you like that, Bob. I'm sorry if you misunderstood my intentions."

"No problem. Let's go and eat." They went inside and Vanessa sat them together by the window.

Over dinner they talked about many things. The schoolwork and how Frank had done on the fluid dynamics test, which he had aced, by the way. They talked about the television show. Even about the long-twisted trip that had brought Bob here.

"I'm still not sure why. Just seemed like the right thing to do. Still does."

"When was the last time you talked to your wife?" Frank asked.

"About eight, or eight and a half years ago, I guess now. I had asked her to send some of my things, like the album and such. She did. She didn't understand what was going on, hell, I didn't, but she knew enough to let me do it."

"Wow." Frank sipped his drink. "Would you talk to her if I could arrange a call?"

"No, son, don't waste your time. Been too long and I heard she had moved on. Don't blame her. She deserves better than this."

"What about you?"

"I'm good, Frank. Believe it or not, I'm good right here."

*   *   *   *

The next few weeks went real quick for Frank. He spent many hours studying for the finals, and then the finals themselves. Each of them was a five-hour marathon test. The only free time he went out of his way to make was Thursdays, for dinner with Bob. He got to know him pretty well over those weeks. He was amazed at the man's mind, but still couldn't really understand why he had given it all up. On the last night he would be in town he had arranged to meet Bob.

"I ship out tomorrow, Bob. I'm really glad I got to know you."

"Me too, I guess," Bob said, adding a playful wink.

"I think I know of a way I can stay in touch, if you're interested," offered Frank. "I could send you a letter here. I checked with them and they said it would be okay. Pick it up when you come in, answer if you like."

"Okay, Frank. We could try that."

When the meal was done and paid for, the two men stood on the sidewalk and said their good-byes. Frank watched from his car while Bob made his way down the street and out of sight. Over the next two years, Frank had sent a dozen letters to Bob, but had never heard back. He didn't even know for sure if Bob ever saw them.

*　　　　*　　　　*　　　　*

The lessons that Bob had shown Frank, about how to think through the mechanics and the problems he would face, stay with him to this day. It's been almost twenty years since they had met in that crazy little restaurant, so far away. There isn't a time that goes by when Frank doesn't see a homeless man, or bottle collector, and doesn't think of Bob, or think about what might have happened to the man. Frank has thought about going back there, to that IHOP, in that far away city, but it is gone. Like the old saying about two ships, these two men shared a time, a magical time together and then drifted away into their own lives. Is Bob still alive? Frank wonders about it and hopes so. Maybe Bob is out there changing someone else's life.

"Hey, mister, what ya' readin'?"

Frank looked up from the table and answered, "Fluid Dynamics."

"I got that next semester," the kid said as he approached the table.

THE END

The Next Level

"Oh, shit," Brian said.

"What? What's up?" I asked.

"Man, this scene with the disemboweling is really insane. I can't believe you think this shit up," Brian said, laughing at the end.

"Better that I write it down and not do it, right?"

"Shit, yeah. Let me know when you think you really want to do some of this, and I'll move to like Montana."

"Who said I haven't done it, and am using it as the inspiration to write?" I asked.

Brian was my editor and he was reviewing the latest of my short stories. I had written a novel and was working on a second one, but I was also trying to get my foot in the door by entering, and hopefully winning, some short story contests. This is the fourth year doing so. I've sent in stories to three contests over the last three years and haven't made the finals. I don't know if that is because I suck, or because they don't like my subject matter. I tend to write serial killer stories that are very graphic and twisted.

"Are you sure that all of the medical stuff is right on?" Brian wanted to know.

"Yeah, I checked with my sister, she's a nurse. I want it to be as realistic as possible, so I always check my facts. I don't need some guy out there reading it and saying, 'Hey, this isn't real'."

"You sure make it sound real."

"I try," I added before taking another sip of my wine.

As we work over the text, we were trying to eat a light dinner. We meet up at the pub and review the story over food and drink. Tonight, we were having Philly-cheese steak heroes and red wine. The French fries tasted a little greasy, so I was trying not to eat too many. I've known Brian most of my life and his expertise in grammar and literature made him the perfect person to help me out.

We finally finished the editing, which as usual, hadn't been that bad. I would like to think of myself as a decent writer and having read thousands of books I feel that I have a pretty good grasp on grammar and sentence structure. Brian, though he reads the story, breaks it down sentence by sentence to ensure that they are correct. He usually just takes out or adds a few commas and breaks up the one or two run-on sentences that he finds. Tonight, was no different, though he did find three partial sentences and I corrected them on the spot.

"I think this is probably the sickest one so far," Brian said as he pushed away from the table to lean back in the chair and enjoy his wine. "I am so glad you like me."

"Thanks, Faye said the same thing. She also told my family that if she ever disappears without a trace, to take the house apart board by board because she's sure that they would find her in it somewhere." That made us both laugh. "She also thinks I'm making sicker story lines, but that I'm writing them better. I guess the quantity of writing is helping."

"Oh, yeah, your dialog and setups are very realistic. I'm sure you're going to hit the right thing real soon. When the people at these contests read your stuff, they should feel the emotions you want them to. That's the whole point, right? Then I think you're doing great. I like reading them, though sometimes I feel like I need a shower after." That made us laugh again, then he added, "Someday I'll be able to say, I knew John when."

I picked up the check and the marked-up story and we made our way outside. Shaking his hand, I thanked him and reminded him that I would be seeing him in three weeks with another story.

*   *   *   *

Faye was shaking me awake. "Honey, you have to see this."

"What's going on? What time is it?" I wanted to know.

"Look at this news story."

I sat up and grabbed my glasses from the nightstand on my right. It was two-thirty-six in the morning. The anchor woman was telling us about how a woman was found murdered tonight. She had been found a few hours ago by her boyfriend. He was now a suspect, but the details of the murder were eerily familiar. I sat up and listened more intently.

"That's fucked up," Faye said taking a hold of my hand.

"Yeah, but why couldn't this wait until morning?"

"Don't you see it? You wrote that last year in one of your stories, the one I liked with the female killer."

"Yeah, but I didn't do this last night."

"I know you didn't, but doesn't seem like the killer had read your story?"

"Honey," I said, "all it means is that this guy came up with something similar to what I wrote. I'm pretty sure that there are only a few ways to kill people and that similarities will always be there when this sort of thing happens."

"You think?"

"Yeah. I mean, it has to be that way." I placed my glasses back on the table, laid back down and pulled the sheet up under my chin. "Good night, again."

Faye leaned over and kissed my forehead, "Sorry I woke you, good night."

I laid there awake for a while before falling asleep again. I couldn't shake what Faye had said. Could whoever killed this woman somehow have read one of my stories? No way. How? Could it be one of the contest people? Doubt it. Brian? Again, no way, he doesn't have the stomach for it. I was trying to consider all the angles and slowly faded away into the night.

*   *   *   *

Brian had called me to say he was running a little late tonight and to start without him. I had just gotten myself a glass of wine and was flipping through the story when he came in. It was a good one, or so I thought. Faye thought it was a little weird because of the hypnosis theme, because she didn't think that hypnosis would work that way. From all of the research I had done, I was pretty sure I was blurring the edges of reality just a little to make it an interesting story, but the basics were there to appease the realists.

As we ate, Brian found a few things in the story that I had to fix. "John, if I could hypnotize people like this...my day would have been so much better."

I laughed and threw in the counter to that. "How do you know that someone hasn't hypnotized you to feel that way?"

That stopped his laugh in mid-breath. For three seconds he just stared at me before realizing I was just fucking with him and then he laughed harder and longer.

With the editing finished, we sat there talking about life and music and work. Out of the corner of my eye I saw something on the television, the news, and the lead story. I stood up and asked the bartender to turn it up for a moment. Brian joined me and we listened as the anchor explained how another woman had been killed today. Again, it was just like another one of my stories. That was now two.

Brian asked, "What's the matter, bud?"

"Doesn't that sound like the story I wrote over last winter?"

"Yeah, a little."

"Just a little?"

"Yeah, I mean, you didn't do it right?"

"Of course not, but a few weeks ago there was another one."

"Another what? Woman killed like this?"

"Well, not like this, but just like in one of my stories." We made our way back to the table and I took a long deep gulp of my wine.

"John, I think you're reading too much into this. People get killed every day and some of them are going to sound just like something you wrote or read." He looked hard at me. "Come on, haven't you've read a book and then heard about some crazy bastard in a documentary that used that as his guideline for his spree. Or worse, read something you thought was the worst thing ever, before hearing on the news that someone had gone way further out there disgusting you, right?"

"Yeah, I guess. I told Faye the same thing. It's just so weird for me. I think this shit up then write it down, but now it's happening."

"Hey, you have nothing to do with what happened tonight, or with the other woman."

"Unless it's because someone read my stories." I took another hit of the wine.

"Like who? Me? Faye? That's a pretty small list, John."

"I guess, but I can't shake this bad feeling I'm getting."

"What do you want to do about it?" Brian asked.

I had no answer for him.

"See, now let's finish our wine and go home to our wives and fuck them silly tonight, okay? And forget about this coincidence. That's all it can be."

"You're right." I downed the last of the Merlot and paid the check. We walked out into the parking lot and said our good nights. I climbed into the car and watched as Brian turned out of the parking lot.

I was in bed and finally almost asleep when I heard Faye say, "Maybe we should talk to the police, hon." Faye was in her 'woman protecting her family' mood. I could understand where she was coming from.

"I just don't know what to tell them. I write stories." I rolled over and faced her in the dark. "They sound just like these killings and I wrote about it first. I can show them the dates the stories were written, but do you think that will convince them?"

"I just think this whole thing is freaky and we should get out in front of it is all."

"Faye, honey. I know you're scared. So am I, but for now I just want to wait it out. Okay?"

"Okay," she said with her mouth, but not her eyes. She kissed me and rolled away from me. I had been dismissed.

*   *   *   *

Knock, knock, knock!
Bang, Bang! "Mr. Donovan?"
Knock, knock!

I rolled over in the bed and rubbed my eyes. "Who the fuck is knocking on my door at this ungodly hour," I say as I sit up, pull on some sweatpants and my glasses, and head towards the door. It was one-twenty-seven in the morning. Faye sat up and looked at me, with that irritated look that she has.

Bang, Bang! "Mr. Donovan?"

"I'm coming, I'm coming. Just hold on will ya," I yelled, my left hand scratching my balls. I got to the door, opened the dead bolt and pulled the door open quickly. "What the hell do you want?" I stopped dead.

The two people on the stoop were holding up gold badges for my inspection, and there were four more uniformed cops standing out on the lawn, their cars were blocking the driveway and part of the street.

"Mr. Donovan?"

"Ah, yeah. What's going on?" I pushed the door fully open and stepped back into the living room allowing the police officers to enter. The two detectives came in, asked me to sit and then they started explaining why they were there.

"Mr. Donovan, I'm Detective Johnson and this is Detective Katt. You're not under arrest, at the moment, but that could change. We have a search warrant to search the premises and…"

"What's going on?" Faye asked as she walked into the room, rubbing her eyes.

"Honey, it's okay. These are Detectives from the police department, and I'm pretty sure they're here about the dead women."

"So, you know about them?" Detective Johnson asked.

"I've seen them on the news and was wondering how long it would take you to get here. I didn't do it, is all I can say. Search all you want, but there's nothing here. I don't know these women, and I sure as hell didn't kill them."

Faye came and sat with me on the couch as the two detectives talked to me. They asked me a lot about my whereabouts on the nights in question. Unfortunately, my wife Faye was my alibi on the first day in question and we all knew that wasn't going to help. The second night though, we had been at a concert with a few friends from work and their spouses. I gave the detectives their phone numbers. I wasn't worried, much.

"We received a call from a Mrs. Rodriguez at the 'Short Story Fiction Contest'. Apparently, it is a writers' contest that you have entered some material into."

"Yes, it is. I've sent in some short stories over the past four years. I agree that they contain material that you will find incriminating because these women have been killed in very similar manners, but I assure you. I only wrote it as fiction. I could never hurt anyone, much less kill an innocent woman."

"Mrs. Rodriguez saw the murders on the news, recognized that they felt somehow familiar, and pulled out some stories and found yours. They were close enough that she gave us a call and forwarded us some copies."

"So, you've read them?"

"Yes, Mr. Donovan, and I must tell you that we are going to take samples of your blood and semen. They will be processed for type, DNA and other essential characteristics that will determine if you were at the scenes of these murders."

"I have no problem with that, Detective, ah, Johnson was it? Whatever it takes to make this not about me. Do I need a lawyer for any of this? If you're not going to arrest me, I take it you are asking me to volunteer the samples willingly, should I get legal advice?"

The two detectives looked at each other for a moment and then Detective Johnson said, "We would advise you to talk to one. We will be taking you with us tonight to get the samples. If you do not want to give them, we will have a court order issued for them to be taken."

"No need for that. I haven't done anything, and I know this will prove it. Faye, can you call Larry Evans when I leave. Tell him what is going on and where we are going."

"Is this Evans guy your usual lawyer? Criminal?"

"He handles a lot of things for us. If he can't help, he'll get me someone who can."

Detective Katt followed me into the bedroom where I got dressed. He made a few suggestions about what I might want to bring with me and what I should probably leave here. I took his advice. I kissed Faye goodbye and reminded her to call Larry right away. She looked worried and I tried to assure her that this would all work out. "I'm not under arrest, honey, they just need to rule me out. Like you see on those television shows. They're always taking the fingerprints of the family members to make sure which sets are theirs and which came from the bad guy." I think she accepted that, but barely. I could tell that she was pissed off.

I spent the next two hours waiting for and then talking to my lawyer who told me that he thought that I should just comply since I was, after all, innocent. So, I did. The police took blood samples, sperm samples, skin samples and a urine sample. They also took teeth impressions and fingerprints. It would take a day or so to get all of the results back, but they assured me that some of the preliminary findings would be back by the morning. They let me go home and I got there exhausted and needing a shower. Faye was sitting up waiting, sipping on a White Russian. She liked those. I told her that everything was fine and headed for that shower. Afterwards, I joined her on the couch with a beer. Boy did that feel good going down.

I looked at the clock and found that it was almost seven in the morning. I called my boss and told him I wasn't feeling very well and wouldn't be in today. He said no problem, told me to get some rest, but that I better be ready for tomorrow. I laughed and said no problem. I remember resting my head on Faye's shoulder for a moment, and then nothing.

*   *   *   *

I was waking up with a pain in my neck, wondering what the hell had happened. I tried to sit up and found that I couldn't. I looked around the room. Faye was sitting in the chair across the room, her head at a strange angle.

"Faye?" I called to her. "Wake up, Faye."

It took a few more moments of calling for her to stir. When she did, she was crying out, struggling against the ropes securing her to the chair. I told her to relax. She looked at me, her eyes blinking rapidly in pain and fear.

"It's okay, honey," I said while trying to put on a brave face, "Just try to relax until we see what's going on, okay. It's me they want."

"How touching," a voice called from the kitchen. "Now, will the two of you just shut the fuck up while I finish eating my breakfast, I don't want to get heartburn."

The voice sounded familiar and Faye and I looked at each other, both of us trying to place it. Faye was also trying to get her left hand free by pulling and then releasing tension on the rope. I could see the skin getting raw and red where it was being abraded.

"Pssst." I hissed. "Stop it."

Faye lifted her head and gave me her patented 'fuck you' look. I left her to it. I had tried pulling on my ropes, but they were too tight, I couldn't get enough of a swing in any direction to do any good. I watched as she continued, finally drawing blood, which dripped onto the carpet below with a steady plip…plip. It didn't seem to slow her down.

The two of us both turned towards the kitchen when we heard the plates, or bowls, clang into the sink. I waited to see who was going to show up, to put the face with the voice. Faye worked harder and faster against her bonds. I smelled cigarette smoke. Whoever was in there was smoking and this would all start when they finished, which I was hoping gave us about five more minutes.

Faye struggled and pulled, gritting her teeth against the pain I knew she was in. Slowly, as I watched, her hand slid under the rope and popped free. Her head whipped to the door and then she started trying to untie her other hand. It took her what felt like to me to be an eternity before the rope fell away. Faye started on the rope around her ankles and within moments it was off, and she was free. She rushed to me and threw her arms around me and kissed me.

"Honey," I whispered, "Get the hell out of here. Don't worry about me. Go a few houses down and call nine-one-one."

She didn't seem to want to hear me. She was starting on my ropes.

"Stop it." I said. "Go. Go now."

She looked at me with fury in her eyes, but I think she got the message. If she got caught here, it was over for both of us. She just might get out and get some help, and that was what she had to do. She kissed me and ran down the hallway towards the bedroom. I knew she would go out the window. I lowered my head, thanking whatever God there is that she was safe.

*　　　　*　　　　*　　　　*

"Ready or not, here I come, you two," the voice called.

I looked up to see Brian enter the room. He was smiling and holding a cigarette in one hand and a large knife in the other.

"Fuck," he yelled when he saw that Faye was gone. "Where'd the bitch go?"

"What the hell are you doing, Brian? What's gotten into you?"

"Into me? You're the one writing all this wonderful sick shit, John." Brian was running around the room and then down the hallway looking for Faye. "Fuck." I heard him yell from the other room. *Good, she was out.* One thing I didn't have to worry about now.

"Brian. I was writing fiction. What have you done?"

"Done? Done?" He flopped down in the chair that used to hold Faye. He took a deep drag on the cigarette, leaned back and blew the smoke out towards the ceiling. "I've given your work the respect it needed. Made it real. Took it to the next logical level."

"Logical level? What the fuck are you talking about? You killed people, Brian."

"Yeah, I guess I have." It seemed like that was the first time he thought about it like that. "But, what the hell. You have to break eggs to have breakfast, or something like that, right?"

He got up and walked over. He took another drag on the cigarette and gently placed the knife point onto my thigh, halfway between my waist and knee. As he was smoking, he started leaning onto the knife. I watched as it made a deep depression and then suddenly popped right into me. The pain was shocking, and I broke out into a sweat immediately. I didn't scream out but watched as the knife disappeared further and further into my leg. Then it stopped. The knife must have come up against the chair and couldn't go any further.

"I thought you were a pretty good writer, John, but when I started reading those stories of yours. Wow. Such magnificence. The way you took murder and sickness and made it all yours. Those television shows our wives watch should have hired you to write for them. You are so much better than the shit they put out."

"Thank you," I said between short breaths trying to keep my sanity. The pain was throbbing, pulsing. The knife was wiggling with each movement of Brian's hand and was sending waves of nausea through me.

"Shut up, you idiot. This isn't about you. You lacked the vision to go to new heights. I'm giving that to you." Without warning, Brian pulled the knife out of my thigh.

"Fuck," I yelled. That hurt more than when it had gone in.

Again, without warning or hesitancy, Brian drove the knife down through my left wrist, pinning my hand to the arm of the chair. This time I screamed.

"There, there. Now you have something to write about. You'll know how the blade feels to better describe the reaction of your characters, your victims."

Brian moved back to the chair and sat down. He smoked and watched me squirm around, as much as the ropes allowed. Blood was oozing out of my thigh and I could feel the warmth spreading out under my ass. I was mesmerized by the glistening knife blade buried in my hand. The dark blood that was pushing past it was very much in contrast to its brightness. I was wondering just how long I could hold on, wondering how long before help would arrive. Would the police believe Faye and come here quickly enough to stop Brian from killing me?

Brian got up and stepped his cigarette out on the rug. He then turned and went back into the kitchen. I heard a drawer open, some rattling, a slam, and then he was back. He had gone for more knives.

"You know something. You said you talked to your sister about the medical stuff. That is so cool. You learned and taught me. And now, I'm going to see if she was telling the truth. We both will."

He took a paring knife, with a blade about three inches long, and pushed it into my abdomen. It hurt, a lot. I was surprised at how easily it had gone in. He pulled it out almost immediately and we both watched as the blood blossomed across my shirt. Brian leaned down and took a deep sniff near the wound. "I don't smell any shit, so I guess she was right." He was laughing. Laughing and pushing the knife into me over and over and over.

The pain had hit some kind of threshold and I was starting to see blackness creeping in from the edges of my vision. My head swooned and I passed out.

Wetness. Cold wetness. I opened my eyes to see Brian standing there holding an empty saucepan. I also felt the cold water across my face, head and chest.

"John, buddy. You gotta do better than that. How are you going to remember how to write about this if you keep falling asleep?" He was laughing at me again. He tossed the pot over his shoulder and it crashed onto the floor and bounced twice before rolling to a stop.

I glanced down and saw a bunch of red spots across my stomach. My left wrist was still impaled to the chair and my thigh was still weeping dark red blood.

"Brian, you have to stop this. You have to…"

"I don't have to stop, John."

"How will I write about it, if I'm dead?"

That stopped him. His head cocked to the side, sort of like when a puppy hears a strange sound. He stood up and walked back the chair and sat down. He placed the knives on the floor and pulled out another cigarette. He lit it with the lighter I was surprised to see that he still had. I had given it to him for Christmas about fifteen years ago.

"Brian," I whispered. My voice was still shaky. "We can work this out together."

"I'm not stupid, John. I'm sacrificing myself for the sake of your art. Your stories will sell like hot cakes after this. We both know that. I'm doing this for you." He picked up one of the knives and threw it at me. It sank deep into my left shin bone.

The sound that came out of me startled both of us. The shriek was like nothing I had ever experienced before. I couldn't stop. I screamed again. Then a third time. Brian got pissed and got up lunging at me. He hit me hard in the mouth. I tasted a thick hot fluid in my mouth and figured that it was blood. He stood there and pulled his right hand back. I looked at him, pleading with my eyes for him not to do this. He shrugged his shoulders and struck me again. My head snapped briskly to the side. I heard a little cracking inside my head.

He hit me over and over. I wasn't sure anymore how many times. My left eye was swollen shut or ruined for good. My lips were split open. The bottom one had had a few teeth go through it. I know I had spit out at least two teeth and that I might have swallowed a third. Blood was flowing freely from my face and dripping down onto my wet, punctured shirt. Finally, he stopped.

I heard the flick of the lighter and raised my head just enough to open my right eye as much as it could to see him sitting in the chair, smoking. His eyes were closed, and the knuckles of his hands were bloodied. His or mine, I wasn't sure. It didn't matter anymore. I tried to speak.

"Brian," the word was slurred, and red spittle followed it out of my mouth. "Don't do this…just go…leave before…they come…go."

"Too late, my friend." He dropped the cigarette butt onto the floor and smashed it out with his boot. He picked up a knife and walked towards me. He was checking the tip with his fingers to see how sharp it was. He leaned down to me, resting his head on my forehead. He stayed that way for a moment and then kissed my head. I had closed my eyes and then I felt his head alongside mine. "I love you, John."

I was about to say something, but I felt his hand slam into my chest. The pain exploded in a white-hot fire all through me. Blinding light, pulsing behind my open eyes was all I could see. I could feel his hands on either side of my head holding me steady. The light was fading, and I could once again sense things in the room. I could see Brian. I could also see the knife handle pressed against my shirt.

Brian stood up. "They'll buy your books now, John."

The room tipped. Or I had. I heard things. Banging. Loud things. Screaming. Well, the screaming might have been me, but I couldn't tell for sure. Things were happening that I couldn't understand at the time. Then hands were all over me. Floating.

*　　　　*　　　　*　　　　*

It took three weeks and many operations to repair what Brian had done to me. It turned out that Faye had gotten to the neighbor's phone and called Detective Johnson. Brian was shot and killed when they came into the house. It also turned out that Brian had killed his wife the night before he tried killing me.

Brian had also been right. Six months after I was out of the hospital my stories were selling like crazy. I had three publishers fighting over my novels, the finished one and the outlines for the next two, and there were multiple television and movie offers. Faye was still trying to protect me by screening the calls and people knocking on the doors. I was finally getting my chance. I hoped that I was up to taking it to the next level.

THE END

Krandall

The Medical Examiner, or ME in the trade, stood by the front door and turned to address the two detectives approaching him through the rain. "Mike," he said, "I hope you guys haven't eaten yet. This is a bad one."

Detective Mike Wallace tossed his cigarette off into the grass, "No problem, Doc, I'm trying to lose a few pounds anyway." The ME and the detective's partner laughed a nervous laugh.

"Listen," the ME added, "it's real messy in there and you need to stay within the marked off areas. Got it?" The crime scene guys were still working collecting evidence and the clear areas were going to be taped off. Everyone knew not to violate the tape and Mike thought it strange for the doc to insist on mentioning it, but once inside he understood. Doc Travis had underestimated his caution. Mike stopped walking and stood quietly, trying hard to not let the vomit inching up into his mouth to come out. He turned his head and stared at the wall for a moment and when he shifted to see if his partner was okay, but saw him quickly exiting the room holding his hand over his mouth.

"Damn, Doc," the detective said, "what the hell went on in here?" There was blood spatter on almost every surface. The carpet was soaked in sections, the walls and ceiling looked like a Pollock painting gone bad, and the furniture was drenched in it. "How many victims are there?"

The ME turned to the detective, "We think there are four, but we'll know more once we start fitting all the pieces back together."

Mike followed the doctor through the scene and listened intently as he described each new atrocity. He stopped a few times to jot down notes on his pad; things that he hoped would help in the investigation.

Apparently, the owner of the house was having some renovations done. The bodies appeared to be those of the contractor and his crew. The owner found them murdered when she arrived home after work and called it in. She was now at the local hospital under observation, the stress and horror had affected her pretty badly. The killer, or killers, Mike was thinking that to overpower four strong construction men, it would have taken more than one accomplice, or a very big gun. Looking at the blood covered saws and hand tools, Mike couldn't help but think about the noise that would have come from this house. Then again, if anyone heard power tools and saw the trucks out front, they would never have assumed that this was what was transpiring behind these doors.

A chop-saw had been used to remove hands, feet, arms and legs from two of the victims. It was surrounded by a puddle of coagulating blood, and the spray pattern emanated about six feet out in either direction from its base. An air-compressed nail-gun had been used to secure feet and hands, and in one case the head, to the floor. One poor bastard had been nailed spread-eagle across a door-opening and then the killer had used a Sawzall to cut through various sections of his body. Mike winced when the doc showed him the coup-de-grace, one of the men had had his testicles and penis nailed to the floor, and the doc was sure that it had been done while the man was still alive.

When the tour was over, Mike thanked the doctor and followed the path back out of the house to find his partner. "Dave," he called when he was near the car, "How you doing?"

Dave Tomlinson looked up at his partner and said, "What the fuck was that?"

"I know, man. I've never seen anything like it either, at least not outside a war zone. You going to make it? You still look a little green."

"Yeah, just caught me by surprise. What did you learn in there?"

Mike lit up a cigarette, something that he was trying to quit, and sat down behind the wheel. He brought Dave up on all his notes, and they talked about what the ME and Mike had surmised about the scene, at least their first impressions. "Had to have been more than one subject   ," Mike suggested.

Dave looked at the notes and asked, "Why do you think that?"

"Come on, four in-shape construction guys taken down by one lone assailant. Hell, Bruce Lee would have had trouble with that."

"Yeah, I guess, but I don't see an extra set of shoes or fingerprints listed here. Maybe Doc Travis can add to this some more." Opening the window, Dave called to the ME who was standing on the front walk talking to the cleanup crew. The ME nodded and was soon making his way to the car. Doctor Carl Travis had been the ME for the last nine years. The detectives had worked with him often over that time and they got along just fine.

Travis dropped into the rear seat and closed the door. "What can I do for you guys?" He patted Dave on the shoulder with that comforting, knowing sign.

"We were just going over the notes and Dave wanted to know if for certain there was more than one assailant in the house. Anything indicating a second bad guy here?"

"Well," Travis started, "as far as me and the guys inside are concerned, there was one perpetrator. We only found one set of bloody shoe prints," he glanced down at his notes, "size eleven, and though we have to wait for all of the comparison prints to be excluded, only one partial print was found. The rest were smudged or covered in so much blood that they lost all of their definition."

Mike made a few quick notes for himself then commented, "So, we're looking for just one very sick mother-fucker."

"Yup, and..." Travis' phone rang, and he answered it. A moment later, "Listen guys, I gotta run. I'll send you my preliminary findings first thing in the morning."

"Yeah, thanks."

They watched as Travis ran though the worsening rain to the ME van and climbed inside.

Mike shook his head, "I need a drink." He started the car and pulled away from the curb and headed into the night.

*   *   *   *

"You want what?" Captain Dwyer asked in an impolite manner. "Are you fucking kidding me?"

Detective Mike Wallace, lowered his head but responded, "We think this is the act of a serial and that the case we carried six months ago, and the case that Matt Wills and Arturo Jiminez are working are all connected."

Captain Dwyer sat down and placed his hands on the desk. "Tell me, in a short-condensed way, why you think this, and you better not be shitting me. Got it?"

Mike started, "If you look at the...," and finished about fifteen minutes later with, "...and with all that said, we think this is the act of one perpetrator, and we want him."

The Captain sat back and closed his eyes. "Well, you make a compelling argument, but before I set you school-girls loose, I want you to get some input from Krandall. Show him what you've got, and if he says it's a serial...it's all yours. Until then, we go about our business as it is now. Understood?"

"Yes, Sir." Mike stood and quickly left the office, not giving the Captain enough time to change his mind. *Krandall*, he thought, *great*.

Jeff Krandall was a detective who should retire. He'd been around since...well, since ever. Mike has been with Homicide for twelve years and Krandall was around a long time before Mike had started. Krandall also knew everything possible about serial killers. Hell, even the FBI had put him up in hotels for weeks at a time to help them out on difficult cases. He was also a recluse and according to office gossip, a drunk. The kind of drunk that would call it a day around two in the afternoon to get a start at tying one on. And maybe the kind of drunk that would show up for three days with the same clothes on because he hadn't made it home yet. One rumor had it that Jeff showed up around midnight once and slept in his car because he said he couldn't remember where he lived. He knew his stuff though. Mike was hoping that he'd find him sober and in a good mood.

"You trying to get us fired?" Dave wanted to know. They were driving across town to find Krandall. They were both drinking coffee and smoking cigarettes. "This guy is fuckin' nuts and now he's holding our career in his hands.

"No way, Dave," Mike said, "We know what we're up against and once Krandall says it's a serial, we'll get control of the whole case. Our two scenes, and Wills' too. There is no downside to this. At worst, we just work the cases we have and prove our case when we solve it." Dave didn't seem convinced, but sat back and relaxed for the rest of the trip.

*　　　　*　　　　*　　　　*

They found Krandall sitting in a diner finishing a plate of what appeared to have been runny eggs and toast. Mike called to him when they entered the place, "Hey, Krandall, you got a moment for us?"

Krandall looked up from his cup with red rimmed eyes, "Sure, got nothin' else pressing."

Great, thought Mike, *he's just off a drunk*. The two detectives dropped into the booth across from Krandall.

"What brings you guys to the bad side of town?"

"Well, Jeff, we caught a case…"

"Good for you. And this affects me how?"

"…and we think we have a serial. Captain Dwyer…"

"A serial?"

"Yeah, and we were asked to let you see the case files. If you think there's a serial, we get control of the multiple cases and lead a larger team."

"So, you want me to tell you what you have, and then leave me out of it? What's in it for me?" Krandall asked. He held up his cup and the waitress started over with a steaming pot to refill it.

"I honestly don't know. You'd be doing the right thing, for us and for the victim's families. If we know we have a common perp, it would make things easier. If you don't want to help, it will just take us a little longer is all." Mike stood up to leave. Dave sat there, his eyes switching between the two talkers. Mike was almost to the door when Krandall called him back.

"I'll look, but don't expect much from a few minutes with some files. Can you leave them?"

"No." Mike dropped the five folders onto the tabletop and sat back down. He waved at the waitress to bring a few more cups of her coffee.

Krandall flipped through the folders, sometimes going back to a previous one. None of the detectives said a word the whole time. Dave and Mike sat looking out the window and waited. Almost an hour later Krandall broke the silence. "You got one perp." He pushed the folders back across the table. "A single white male, forty to forty-five years old. Lives alone and drives an average type car or SUV. Socially adept to hide his desires, but these three cases aren't the only ones he's involved with."

"You mean there are more?" Dave asked, setting down his cup to start taking notes.

"Yeah, there are more. Five or six others at least. He didn't start out with this level of complexity or ferocity. He worked his way up the sicko ladder to get here. If not in this county, try ones a hundred or so miles away. He might have moved to get out from under suspicion where he used to live. Now, can I finish my breakfast in peace?"

"Just a few more questions," Mike said opening the second folder. "What made you decide so quickly?"

"Well," Krandall said, "You wouldn't have come here if you weren't certain. I saw similar-styled events. All three were crimes of opportunity, so don't go looking for some common event or place linking these victims. The odds of having two sickos like this in one area are pretty low, but you already knew that. You don't need me holding your hand." Krandall reached into his coat and pulled out a flask and poured a good amount of what it contained into his coffee. "You going to turn me in?" he asked with a smile.

"We'll let you know how it turns out, Jeff."

"No need, I'll see it on the news." They were dismissed.

When they were back in the car, Mike and Dave compared their notes and listened to the tape again. Mike knew that he had better have a record of the discussion. *Now the hard part.* They headed back to the office to talk to the captain.

"What took you so long?" Captain Dwyer asked when they walked into his office. "Krandall called a while ago and asked if he could take part in this. I told him that it was up to you. You'd be leading the investigation, and I told him I was sure he'd be hearing from you when the time came."

"Thanks, Captain, that was quick."

"You got what you asked for, guys, so get out there and don't make me regret this decision." The captain got up and passed the detectives on his way out of his office.

*   *   *   *

Cathy was having a hard time getting her mother, who was in a wheelchair, up the walk while carrying the two bags of groceries. She was making progress by using her hips and elbows, but it was not going well. Cathy stopped for a moment and cursed at the sky, "Why me?"

"Who you talking to?"

Cathy whipped around and found a man standing right behind her.

"Here, you take the bags and get the door, I'll drive your mother," he offered.

Cathy was hesitant, but thought that the man looked decent enough, so gave in. Her mom swiveled around to see who was pushing her and gave the man a big smile and a thank you.

The man waited patiently, commenting on the lovely flowers in the garden as Cathy fought to get the door open. She placed the bags inside and turned to get her mother only to find the man had already turned the chair and was effortlessly lifting her mother up the six stairs that were there. She backed up to let him enter the room. As she did so, she watched helplessly as the man turned, and saw his fist rising quickly to catch her right in the left eye. Cathy staggered back and reached for the wall, but the man was on her, driving her to the floor and cracking her head on the hard wood two, three and four times until her vision faded.

"What's going on?" Cathy's mom was asking.

The man turned to her, placed a hand on both sides of her head and quickly spun it around so that she could see for herself. The loud crack of her vertebrae echoed from down the highly polished hallway. When he released her head, it fell limply to the side, her lifeless eyes clouding, and a little trail of spittle dripped from her loose lips to pool on the shiny floor. He glanced outside to see if anyone had noticed the commotion, and seeing nothing, closed the door.

*　　　　*　　　　*　　　　*

The Medical Examiner walked Detective Mike Wallace and the other three detectives through the scene. "Mike, she was still alive for a lot of this. He had opened her and was doing things to her insides while she watched. By removing her eyelids, she had no choice."

"Fuck, man, that's cold," Detective Wills commented.

"I believe that her mother was dead prior to any of her damage. Her broken neck suggests that she went quickly, and he might have done it to keep her quiet." The ME flipped some pages. "He might have made...Mrs. Bartholomew watch. The ligature marks on her ankles and wrists suggest that she struggled violently for a while."

"Why them?" asked one of the detectives.

Mike Wallace, the lead detective answered that. "They had just gotten home with the groceries, which are still leaning on the wall by the front door. The perp helped get the mother up the stairs. I don't think he knew them. He saw her struggling with the wheelchair and offered to help, taking full advantage of the situation."

"That means he must appear normal on the outside." Dave added, "There's no way a woman would let a strange man who looked scary touch her mother or open the door to her house for him."

"Yes, by all accounts, this guy could be anyone and be anywhere and not set off any alarms to those around him. Until it was too late."

The blood had pooled on the floor, the beads were black against the white oak planks. "Mrs. Bartholomew," the ME continued, "had most of her internal organs removed and they're scattered around the room. We think they're all here, so no trophies. He used knives and other cutlery from the kitchen, nothing of his own."

One of the detectives commented, "That again is a means of opportunity."

"Exactly," Mike and Dave said in unison.

"The amount of blood indicates that she was alive for a lot of it. Very little arterial spray, so he was careful, or lucky."

Mike stopped the ME. "Would that indicate he might have had a medical background?"

"Not necessarily, he could have been a hunter. He was butchering her. He might have done that before and knew which areas to avoid."

A few more questions later, the detectives had all that they needed for now. As they turned to leave, Dave stepped in a coagulating puddle and slipped, falling hard onto his back.

The four detectives spread out to the neighboring homes and questioned the occupants, looking for and hoping that someone had seem something that would point them to this guy. None of them noticed the dark car at the end of the adjoining street, idling.

Detective Jeff Krandall took a sip from his flask and lit another cigarette. He knew that the detectives would come up empty for the same reason the killer picked this neighborhood. Everyone here stayed to themselves. There were long driveways or hedged yards, heavy curtains on every window and no grills in the backyards. The killer knew he would be safe. He looked around surveying the streets. *Where would the perp have left his car? Would it be noticed?* He put the car in gear and pulled around the corner. Two blocks later he pulled to the curb and picked up his cell phone.

Mike Wallace and Dave Tomlinson looked at the tire tracks. It felt right. A break. Mike called the crime scene guys to come check it out. Then he turned to Krandall, "What were you doing out here?"

"Hey, I heard it on the radio and wanted to see the scene. I didn't want to intrude, but if you would share your notes, I might be able to help."

"How'd you know to look here for the car tracks?" Dave asked.

"What is this, tag-team cops? I looked for where I would have left my car where no-one would think anything about it. Why didn't you?" He flicked his cigarette butt out into the street and turned to climb back into his car.

"Hey, come on, guys," Mike said, "We're all on the same side here and want the same thing. I have no problem with you checking things out, but why didn't you let us know you were here? Why not go inside the house?"

"I was inside before you guys got here. Seen it."

"Oh?"

"Yeah, when I drove by, I saw a cop I knew from back when and asked for a quick run through. Don't worry, I didn't touch anything, or take anything."

"I know you wouldn't. Never crossed my mind." Mike lied. "What do you think?"

"Probably the same as you." He took a moment to light another cigarette. "This guy drives around looking for easy targets. He saw the minivan with the chair lift. Knew that he had a few minutes to lose the car and get back. Told you. He's a man of opportunity. Took his time inside knowing he wouldn't be interrupted. Enjoyed his time."

"Yeah, a little too much," Dave said.

"Though one thing bothers me." Krandall said. The other two detectives waited for him to continue.

When he didn't, Dave asked, "And that is?"

Krandall looked at him like he was just asked why the sky was blue by a second grader. "He had to have left prints somewhere. He had to take off his clothes and clean up before he left. No way a man could walk down the street, even in this neighborhood, all covered in blood. Couldn't risk a passing car seeing him. So, either there are prints there, or he doesn't have any."

"We agree." Mike liked that Krandall, as far out of it as he was, was still sort of on the game. "He only left smudges at the last two scenes. Nothing usable."

"Well, when you get one, you'll have him. No way this guy ain't in the system."

With that he got into the car and pulled away. Mike let him go. No use questioning him further now. The crime guys showed up a few minutes later and Mike and Dave left them to it.

*   *   *   *

Mike sent the crime scene guys back to all of the previous locations. "Find me a fingerprint," was all he instructed them to do.

It had turned out that the tire marks found by Krandall were from one of the most common types of tires used on vans, light trucks and SUV's. That pretty much narrowed it down to every other house in the county and the five or six neighboring ones as well. As predicted, there were no common threads between the victims, other than the fact that they were killed by the same guy. Interviews with possible witnesses turned up nothing.

Captain Dwyer listened to the report then sat back in his chair, folded his hands behind his head and said, "Just tell me that you got more than that. That we're double-checking a few potential subjects?"

Mike shook his head. The captain scanned the other faces in the room and got similar responses.

"This is not what I expected when I put you on this, Wallace."

"I know, Sir..."

"I wasn't finished."

"...sorry."

"What does Krandall have to say about any of this?" Captain Dwyer asked. "You have brought him in on this, right?"

"Yes, Sir, but he still sort of... you know... we've talked and we all agree about most of what we have. Krandall likes working in his own dark world and it's hard to get him to join a team like this." The captain nodded his head in agreement. *At least he understood*, thought Mike. "He thinks a lot different than the rest of us, and I'm hoping that will work out for the better in the long run. The four of us are headed in the quote-unquote normal directions while Krandall does…well, whatever he does."

"Okay, then don't let me hold you up. We need this resolved quickly and without undue negative publicity."

In the hallway, Mike sent Matt and Arturo back to the last scene. "There's got to be something there. Pull the walls down if you have to."

Mike and Dave were walking when one of the crime scene techs ran up to them. "We have a print. We're running it through the system now. If he's there, we'll know in a few hours." He handed Mike a printout of the print. It didn't look any different than any other print they've ever seen.

"Where was it found?" asked Dave

"Believe it or not, on the inside edge of the silverware divider. One of the other techs said to go over everything and we found it. It's not from the family or the contractors."

"Good work. Let's hope it's him and not some cousin who visited last summer."

*   *   *   *

"This guy is scary, Mike," Dave said as they stood in the front yard of the latest scene. There were two bodies inside that had been brutally taken apart. "This mother-fucker is way out there. You can't convince me no-one knows who it is. He's got to be screwing up in his regular life now."

"I agree." Mike was looking over his notes. The ME had just finished walking them through the scene. The man had had his throat cut and the killer had placed a bandage around it to control the rate of blood loss. Sort of like a tourniquet. His eye lids were removed, like the sicko had done on the woman last week, only this time it was so he could watch his wife be assaulted by the bad guy. She had been beaten by a baseball bat that the killer had found in one of the closets. Most of her bones had been broken and for all intents and purposes she looked like one big bruise. The husband had only suffered one other physical injury. He had been eviscerated, while still alive. His intestines were piled up all around his feet.

Krandall pulled up and walked over to the detectives. "I hear it's real bad in there." He got a nod from the others and proceeded inside to see for himself. When he returned, he stood to the side with Mike and Dave and lit up a cigarette. "I think this guy is close to coming unglued." He watched for the agreement from the others. "Anybody see his truck?"

"No." Dave glanced around for somewhere to toss his coffee cup, and finding none, drained the cold fluid into the garden, crushed the cup and placed it in his outer jacket pocket.

Across the street, fifty-six-year-old Jennifer Boyle, watched the activity through her curtains and through the cellophane wrapping that was bound around her head. Behind her and breathing down her neck was the killer. He was watching the police and took notice when Krandall had arrived. It was at that moment that Jennifer felt the knife penetrate her kidney. The woman bucked and moaned in his arms, but he held tight, forcing the knife into her over and over again. The blood was making her wet and warm as it flooded inside her clothing. She died looking at the ones who could have saved her had they only known she was there.

Krandall was lighting a second cigarette when he caught the motion across the street. The curtain had moved. No one had answered the door to that home when the officers had canvased the area earlier. He nodded towards the house and the other detectives turned to look where he was indicating. He told them what he had seen, and the three men fanned out. Halfway across the street, Dave called to two of the uniformed police officers to join them. Dave and the two police made their way to the back of the house. Mike and Krandall walked up the stoop. The front porch extended fully across the house. Mike inched towards the first window and peered inside. What he saw made him snap his head back.

"He's right there…" he started, but before he could complete the sentence Krandall burst through the front door. Mike jumped to catch up, but was too late. Krandall and the killer were standing face to face in the middle of the room. Mike froze. Krandall and the killer. It was like looking at a clone. They were identical.

Mike heard movement and looked down the hallway to see the others approaching with weapons drawn.

"Who are you?" Krandall asked.

"Apparently, I am you, and you are I."

"Put the knife down," Mike instructed the man.

The killer raised his eyes as if seeing Mike for the first time. With a quick flick of his wrist, the knife hand came up and slashed across Krandall's throat. The blood spray arced three feet in two directions. Krandall didn't move. He grabbed the killer by the shirt front and pulled him nose to nose. For a moment, nothing happened. Then the two men slowly sank to the floor. When their knees touched the carpet, a loud boom filled the quiet that had enveloped the room. Krandall's gun had fired, blowing a hole in below the killer's chin and the top of his head blew off, spray-painting the ceiling with blood and brain matter.

The detectives and officers rushed forward to find both men dead, entwined in a macabre mirror-like embrace. A moment later Mike received a text message from the crime lab that the prints belonged to Jeff Krandall.

*   *   *   *

Two days later Detective Jeff Krandall was laid to rest with full honors. The killer, Byron Kelly as it turns out, was buried by his family in an unmarked grave.

"Krandall never knew that he had a brother." Mike was telling the captain. "Their mother didn't want to or couldn't raise both, so she put one up for adoption."

"Wow," Captain Dwyer said, "Nature or nurture thing, right. Maybe Jeff would have become a killer as well had he not learned to channel those feelings into law enforcement."

"Maybe that's why he was so good. He really could think like them. Scary, huh?"

"For all of us."

The rifle shots echoed through the afternoon. Three volleys of seven. As Mike, Dave and the captain were heading for their cars, Mike's cell phone rang.

"Yeah…," they looked at each other, "we're on the way."

THE END

Lost and Found

"Fuck!"

The rain did nothing but add to the depression. Jim Spencer needed a break, a vacation. The last time off that he had taken was when his mother had died, almost five years ago. He was driving to the family cabin that was nestled in the woods, on a lake at the top of a quote-un-quote mountain in lower New York State. Working six days a week and close to seventy hours, was more than Jim could take right now. His last performance review didn't go quite like Jim had hoped. Almost every category showed that he had needed some improvement, which was bull shit of course. He worked his ass off. Jim was nearing forty-five years old and he was tired of being fucked over, so he took a two-week leave.

Adding to his misery was his girlfriend, Diane, the bitch. They had been dating for close to two years now and Jim thought that things were progressing nicely. He was actually thinking, that maybe on a long weekend during the upcoming summer, of popping the question. Then about a month ago, Diane shows up very early on a Saturday morning, un-announced.

That wasn't the problem. The problem was that she had brought some guy with her. A fucking guy, to Jim's place, to gather up her things. They were apparently done with and Jim hadn't yet gotten that memo.

Fog started crossing the road in thicker bands causing Jim to slow down. The windshield wipers were already going on full blast, clacking back and forth, trying to keep the glass clear enough for Jim to at least see the road. He pulled out a cigarette and lit it. The smoke wafted around the car's cabin on the breeze created by the defroster. Jim took a long drag on the butt, secretly wishing that he had a drink to go with it, felt its heat in his throat and then let it out slowly through his nose. *Much better.*

After a longer drive than Jim had planned, or had hoped for, he pulled the car to a stop under the carport alongside the cabin. He killed the engine, but sat there in the new silence to finish the cigarette he was enjoying and to breathe a sigh of relief that he had made it. Too much stress on the road was giving Jim a headache, which was the last thing he needed to cap off such a wonderful month.

After entering the cabin, Jim made his way to the bedroom and tossed his bag onto the bed causing a small puff of dust to poof into the air. There were cobwebs on pretty much every surface. Nobody had been here since last fall and it showed. Jim plugged in the refrigerator and put the food stuff away, then he looked in the cabinets for the coffee maker. First things first. The bourbon would be better served if he waited to start that in the evening. He was going to be spending two weeks here, so he had plenty of time to fry his brain cells.

He dug through one of the closets and came up with an older towel and used that to wipe down a lot of the common surfaces that he would be using like the counter tops, sinks, toilet seats and tables. He could smell the coffee and knew that it was ready. He found a good-sized cup, filled it, and then made his way to the living room where he turned on the television that he knew only received three stations on a good day. Today wasn't one of those days. *No surprise there.* The only thing Jim could find on it was a local station playing a very fuzzy afternoon soap. He shut the set off and plopped down onto the couch and closed his eyes.

*　　　　*　　　　*　　　　*

Jim's first thought was that he should have started a fire before nodding off. He woke up coughing and freezing. When he opened his eyes, Jim found himself under water, cold and oppressive water. The light seemed so far away as Jim's mind tried frantically to get this body moving, but all he did was float ever further from the light. Jim could see the waves on the lake's surface rippling, making shadows dance feverishly around him. Coughing again, Jim's body finally responded, and he flailed his arms trying desperately to break the surface.

When Jim was almost to the top, his hands mere inches from freedom, Jim felt something, maybe a hand, grab his ankle. In panic, Jim launched himself up and away to find hands grabbing his shirt and arm.

Jim tried to push the unwanted hands off of him, but they held fast. Jim felt himself being lifted from the water and then the hard surface of the old wooden dock cut into his back.

"Are you okay?"

Jim tried to answer, but could only nod and cough the fluid out of his lungs. He felt a hand rubbing his and another one was lying on his shoulder as his body wracked itself to dispel the intruding water. A moment later he tried to sit up and got to see his rescuer for the first time.

"Take it easy," the woman said, "you've had a rough thing just happen."

"I'm okay," Jim managed to squeak out. Jim's red swollen face, bloodshot eyes and coughing told a different story.

"What happened?" the woman asked.

"I'm not sure." More coughing, and then he added, "I was sleeping on the couch and suddenly found myself in the water."

"Were you drinking?"

"No. And what the hell kind of question is that?"

The woman reached into her pocket and pulled out a sheriff's badge.

Great. One more thing to add to the list. "Sorry. No, I wasn't drinking. You'll find a half empty cup of coffee on the table next to the couch, promise."

"I believe you. Maybe you sleepwalked out here." The sheriff added by way of explanation to herself and to Jim. "Ever happen to you before?"

"This would be a first, I think."

"I'm Sheriff Bridget Handler, by the way."

"Jim Spencer. I'm staying in the family cabin right there." Jim stood and rubbed his hands over his cooling arms. "Can we talk about this inside so I can get a towel or something?"

"Sure."

The two of them made their way to the cabin. As Jim left to find a towel, Sheriff Handler looked around. She noticed the unopened suitcase on the bed, a cold half a cup of coffee on the table, and no booze in sight. Maybe Jim was telling her the truth after all. Jim returned carrying the suitcase and rubbing a towel over his head and neck.

"If you don't mind," he said while dropping the towel and opening the suitcase to find a dry shirt to put on.

"Not at all."

"Thanks for pulling me out of there. Was very brave of you."

"No problem. I was passing by and noticed all the splashing. By the time I got to you, you were almost out on your own."

Jim moved to the fireplace and started setting up a few logs and kindling to get some heat flowing through the space. In a few moments, small flames were licking at the larger pieces and spreading out nicely.

"That should help," Sheriff Handler added.

"So, what were you doing way out here, if you don't mind me asking?"

Sheriff Handler snorted a little laugh and turned towards Jim. "I figured no one was out here, so I come to run around the water. Helps me to clear out my head."

"Well, I'll be staying here for a week or so, feel free to stop by on your runs."

Bridget smiled, "Thanks. Maybe I will."

Jim poked a log with the poker, and it spat back at him. He was considering asking the sheriff if she wanted a drink or something. Was it proper? Would he look foolish?

"Well, I gotta get going. Places to go and all that. I hadn't planned on spending this much time on this side of the lake. It was nice meeting you."

Jim stood and followed her to the door. Shaking his hand, Sheriff Handler said, "I'll check in on you in a day or so. Make sure you haven't drowned." The last was added with a smile.

"I'd like that."

Jim stood in the doorway and watched as the woman trotted across the grass to the water's edge. She didn't look back. Jim hadn't expected her to, but he would have liked it if she had.

The fire did little to heat up Jim's body after his dip in the icy water. He went to the kitchen and grabbed a glass and poured some single barrel bourbon into it. Taking a big gulp, he walked back to stand in front of the fireplace to think further about the afternoon's events.

Jim remembered the drive up. He could account for every moment of opening the cabin and getting it set up, so to speak. He pictured each room in his mind as he walked through them, remembering the food, the cleaning, the coffee, the nap, and then absolutely nothing. Until the water that is. He could remember the water. There was something about the water that wasn't coming to him. Jim knew that there was something more under the surface, no pun intended. It nagged at the back of his skull like an itch that he couldn't get his fingers on.

The bourbon gone, and Jim feeling a little tired, he tossed three more logs onto the fire to insure there would be heat through the night. He then made his way to the kitchen and put together a sandwich from the supplies he had brought and carried it to the bedroom. Jim kicked off his shoes and sat up against the headboard to finish the sandwich. The fresh meat and cheese tasted good and it dawned on Jim that he hadn't eaten anything since that morning.

As the darkness surrounded him, Jim thought about a girl's face. She was pretty and Jim had a feeling that she was from his past. He couldn't place her decided that it was only from a dream. Something about her though. Her, and the water.

*   *   *   *

Jim couldn't move. It was dark and there was a pressure all over his body. He felt something dropping on his face and tried to brush it off, but he could only get one of his hands to respond. He tried breathing and got a mouthful of something hard and tasting nasty. There was a soft breeze on his face, but that only served to scare him more. He pushed with the free hand and only managed to knock more dirt into his own face. He moved it and wiggled it harder, faster. *Holy shit! I'm being buried alive.* Jim struggled, twisted and moved for what seemed like hours to get free. He was grunting noisily against the fear and the night as he made the slow progress.

He had been under only a few inches of the dirt, but the weight over his body limited not only his movement, but his breathing. As Jim struggled, the fear drove his heart rate up and breathing in the dirt caused more pressure in his head. When he was truly free, the scream that drove from his chest was primal and shook the trees all around him. He gasped for breath and lie there on the damp ground until his breathing was back to normal.

When Jim stood up and started brushing the dirt from his clothing, he saw with the help of the moonlight that he was only a few hundred feet from the cabin. He staggered back in that direction trying to figure out what the hell was going on with him. *Okay, you might have sleepwalked off the pier this afternoon, but you sure as shit don't bury yourself.* Jim locked the door behind him and walked hesitantly through the cabin checking in every nook and corner. *Obviously, someone had been here, right? How did they get in? More importantly was who?* Jim poured some more bourbon and kicked the fire up by dropping in a new log for the flames to feast on. He pulled a chair over to sit directly in front of the much-needed heat. *And fuck! What about the why?*

Jim sat there most of the night sipping on the bourbon and poking at the fire. Images appeared and faded as the time went by. A girl's face seemed to show often, but Jim couldn't remember if it was the same face as from earlier. Other images, darker images came and went. Knives, rushing water, total blackness. What did it all mean? Jim eventually pulled his tired body over to the bed and dropped off into a fitful sleep, while debating on whether or not to call the sheriff in the morning. *And tell her what, stupid? That you woke up in the woods burying yourself with no recollection on how you got that way?*

*　　　　*　　　　*　　　　*

The smell of coffee filled the kitchen as Jim cut up the banana to put in his cereal. The night had left him hungry and tired. Lying in bed seemed like the perfect way to spend the day, so it was a good thing he had packed a few books. He had gotten up this morning and still tasted the dirt from the night before, so Jim quickly striped and took a long hot shower. His clothes remained in a pile at the foot of the bed, something for him to worry about tomorrow.

As he ate his cereal, Jim replayed the night before slowly in his head. The fire, the sandwich, going to bed and then waking up buried. No matter how he replayed it, there was something missing. A big piece of the puzzle was eluding him. How the hell did he get out there? The girl's face also added to the dilemma. He knew her, or had to, right? How else would that face be so familiar to him? How was she involved in all of this?

Jim opened his eyes and found that he had been asleep on the bed. By the light through the window, he guessed that it was late afternoon. He lay there deciding what to do when he heard the knocking. He sat up and listened harder. More knocking. Jim got up and answered the door while wiping his eyes, hoping to wake up some more.

Sheriff Handler was at the door. "Good afternoon, Jim, or is it good morning?" Her laugh brought a smile to his face.

"Sort of took a nap, you know, vacation and all." Jim said as a way of explanation.

"I noticed a pretty big messy hole just a ways from here. You burying a raccoon or something?" She was joking of course, but the question took Jim by surprise.

"I, uh, hadn't noticed. I haven't been outside today."

"May I come in?"

"Oh, yeah, sure. What an idiot. Drink? I think I only have some sodas and bourbon."

"Bourbon works."

After some small talk the sheriff asked Jim straight out. "Is there something you want to tell me? Seems like you have been here two or three days and crazy stuff has been happening the whole time."

"I can see how you could think that, but really, I'm just here to rest. I can't explain it either."

"So, something is going on?"

"That's not what I meant."

"Well," she stood up, placed the glass on the table and walked towards the door. "I'll be checking in more often now, so if you change your mind." She turned and left before Jim could respond.

Jim gulped the last of the bourbon in his glass and almost threw the glass into the fireplace. That would have been the dramatic thing to do, but at the last second, he remembered that they were crystal glasses. He put the glasses in the sink and walked out to look at the hole again in the fading evenings light. It was a small shallow grave. It looked like one. It was almost his own. *But why? Why was I trying to bury myself?*

Jim took his time walking back to the cabin and looked at everything he could see. Was anything out of place? Not that he could remember. The path, the dock, the cabin and his car all seemed the same to him. He should try to pay better attention to his surroundings and maybe this sort of shit wouldn't happen to him…again.

*   *   *   *

Jim spent the day sitting on the front porch in one of the lounge chairs. Something to drink, a book to keep his mind away from the issues and he was set. As the sun got hotter, Jim removed his shirt to get a little color on more than just his arms.

The girl's face was in front of him and as the angle of view changed, he could see the hands wrapped tightly around her neck. The girl was struggling, but the hands held fast. Her face turned from flesh, to red, and to blue and then Jim's eyes snapped open. The book leapt from his lap and the glass smashed on the flagstone when it tumbled from the table.

Jim got up and ran. At first, he was covering his eyes from the images they had just witnessed, but that caused him to stumble and fall across the grass. He got up slowly and walked deeper into the woods. Tears were in his eyes. *Why is this happening to me?* Aimlessly he kept going trying to put more distance between him and the nightmare from the cabin.

When he finally stopped, Jim found that the cabin was out of sight and that he didn't recognize where he was. *Great.* He turned around slowly hoping to find something of a beaten path to follow back, but he found none. Jim figured that if he turned around, sooner or later he should hit the lake and be able to find the cabin.

The walk back seemed to take forever and was very painful. Jim had run off the porch without anything on his feet. On the run out he didn't seem to notice, but now, every stick and stone seemed to be finding just the right place to hit. Swearing and stepping lightly, Jim almost didn't notice that the ground cover had turned to the grassy lea surrounding the water. Looking around he figured that he was a lot further from the cabin then he had thought. Jim turned to his right and started the long walk home, glad that it was finally much easier on his feet.

Jim couldn't get the image of the girl out of his head. She had such a pretty face and being tortured like that by those hands must have been horrible. Those hands looked big and strong, like clamps around her poor little neck, crushing it and the life from her. Jim looked down at his hands. Was his imagination playing games on him, or did they sort of look like the ones in those visions? He kept trying not to think about it, but they stayed in his vision as he walked and therefore his mind.

The bourbon burned all the way down to his stomach, but Jim needed it bad. The sour taste followed, and he almost threw it back up, but gulped a few times to keep it down. Another hit of the bourbon and he sat on the couch, at the front edge of the cushion. He closed his eyes trying to force the images and thoughts away, but they were right there, taunting him. The girl's face in a few positions swirled around.

The hands open, the hands closed on a fragile neck, the hands holding a knife that jabbed up and down continuously, getting bloodier each time and then starting clean again.

Jim cupped his head in his hands and started crying which led to sobbing. The forgotten glass dropped from his hand to roll on the floor. The sobs wracked Jim's body and he slid to the floor to kneel in the wet spot. Leaning back against the couch the sobs continued. They also brought back clearer pictures, like memories. The girl's faces each were different, all three of them. Three girls have died and somehow, they are connected to Jim, and now he thought he understood.

His younger days are a blur of broken images. A bad car accident at the age of twenty-six had left Jim broken with multiple fractures and head injuries. Some of his memories have never come back. Until maybe right now. This weekend. Jim's head whirled at the implications. *Had he been a killer before the accident? Did he really kill these three girls? Were there more out there?*

Jim looked around the cabin. He had been here many times growing up. Is this where it had happened and why the memories had come back now? Jim got up and started tearing things apart, knocking things off of the shelves to see if there were hidden panels. He went up into the attic and tossed every box he could find. He dug through every corner and thankfully came up empty. He made his way back to the couch and dropped exhausted onto it. Sweat dripped from his head and arms. He could feel it winding its way down his sides and across his back. Jim started laughing.

*   *   *   *

Jim looked at Carol and smiled. She was cute. He knew he would be taking her out tonight. He drove up to the lake where he knew they would be alone. The stroll under the moonlight was romantic. They sat on the edge of the dock and talked and kissed. Then Jim knocked her into the water. She was surprised and he laughed. He reached down as if to help her and she grabbed for the offered help. Jim pulled Carol a little closer, leaned over the water, took a hold of her by the neck and forced her head back under the water.

Carol screamed large bubbles of air and sucked in the cold silent water in reply. Jim tightened his grip while holding Carol's head just below the surface. He wanted to watch her eyes in the bright silver light. Such lovely blue eyes they were. Carol's hands found Jim's and struggled, but his grip was too strong. He looked into those precious eyes until the water became calm. Then Jim held Carol under the water longer to remember those eyes forever.

It took some effort for Jim to get Carol out of the water. He lay her on the dock and then sat back to have a cigarette and enjoy the sight. After a little while, when the cigarette was a memory, Jim picked Carol up and carried her about a hundred yards into the woods. He had a spot all ready where he would bury her and visit every time that he was at the cabin.

*   *   *   *

Jim remembered it all now. "Holy Shit!" he yelled at the ceiling when his eyes snapped open. He jumped up and started for the door. He stopped and ran back to the kitchen to grab a flashlight. He was sure he didn't need it. He knew the way.

*   *   *   *

Nichole sat at the counter in the coffee shop and Jim made sure to make eye contact. She soon noticed and smiled back. When he got up to leave, he noticed that she watched him go. She was primed. He sat in the car and waited. Sure enough, Nichole came out to get into hers. It wouldn't start. Jim had made sure of that. As he pulled away, she made eye contact again, the 'I need help' kind so Jim stopped and offered her a ride.

As soon as they pulled out of the parking lot, Jim hit Nichole very hard in the side of the head driving it into the glass. Over and over he hit her, harder and harder until she stopped moving. She wasn't dead, because he could still see her breathing. He drove to the cabin, smoking and singing on the way. He occasionally looked over to make sure that his victim was still out. He parked the car on the side of the house and lifted Nichole out. She wasn't as heavy as Carol had been. Jim wondered if that was because she was dry, and not saturated with all the water from the lake.

Nichole lay still as Jim dug the shallow grave just a few yards away from Carol's. He could see weeds and dandelions were starting to grow on Carol's grave and smiled. When the hole was deep enough, he put

Nichole in and waited for her to come around. He wanted…no…he needed…her to be awake. When she started to stir, Jim removed his clothes and climbed into the hole with Nichole, taking a seat on her thighs.

"What? What's going on? What happened?"

"It's okay Nichole. I'm here."

"Who the fuck are you? Hey!"

Jim pulled the large hunting knife out of the scabbard at the small of his back. The moonlight reflected off of it making it look scarier than it was. Or so he thought. Nichole didn't say one way or the other. As fear blossomed in Nichole's eyes, Jim slammed the knife down penetrating Nichole's chest. It was harder to do than what it looked like in the movies and the knife didn't go all that deep. Nichole started screaming, so Jim slammed the knife down again, and again. Over and over he smashed it through her ribs and organs. The blood, having started out pumping, now only trickled. The life in Nichole's eyes was long gone.

Jim was covered in blood and knew that a dip in the lake would wash it away. He slowly stood, admired his work and proceeded to cover the still oozing body of Nichole. The water cleared the blood, which looked very dark, almost black in the moonlight, leaving Jim clean, refreshed and very cold. He dried himself off, got dressed and then walked back over to where the graves were and stood until the sun came up, wondering about his next placement.

*　　　　　*　　　　　*　　　　　*

Jim did remember the way and was soon standing in the small clearing. It looked familiar. There were seven depressions where wildflowers were starting to pop up. Jim stood still, shocked by the ramifications. He was frightened, and yet somehow overjoyed. He had returned and so did his full memory. He knew each depression and each of the pretty young faces that they hid. He switched his gaze from one to the next while whispering each of their names *"Lisa, Debra, Nichole, Carol...Lucy"*

*　　　　　*　　　　　*　　　　　*

Sheriff Handler was approaching Jim Spencer's cabin when she noticed him running off into the woods. She killed the lights and pulled the cruiser off to the side of the road. She had known that there was something going on that first day, even if Jim Spencer refused to tell her. She checked her weapon, climbed out of the car and started following the bobbing light. He had a minute head start in the woods, but she kept pace with the image in front of her while trying to make sure that in the dark she didn't run into something or worse, sprain an ankle.

*　　　　　*　　　　　*　　　　　*

Jim sank to his knees and started tearing at the ground in front of him, pulling clumps of grass and tossing them aside and using the flashlight to dig down through the old tamped dirt. He cleared the loosened debris and was soon looking at the face of his sister. Everyone in the town, county and state believed that she had run away, and she was still listed on the missing persons' wall at the local police station. Their parents went to their graves believing it also, broken by the thoughts that they had forced her away.

There was a time when Jim was dying and then recovering that they all sort of forgot about Lucy. Now, Jim remembered and wept at the sight of his sister's decomposing face. It was mostly bone with a few traces of mummified skin and hair. Jim picked it from the brittle neck with a small tug and snap and sat back holding it in his hands.

Lucy had been his first. It started as a test, to see how far he could go, he punched her and then beat her until she stopped moving. Fearing what to do, he hid her in a tarp under the crawlspace. They all cried for her and looked everywhere for Lucy, but she was never found. She had finally run away. It was the early 70's and kids were doing it all over the country. She wasn't the first or the last to do so. Time and deaths have made her almost a footnote now.

*　　　　　*　　　　　*　　　　　*

Sheriff Handler arrived and waited. She saw Jim looking over the scene and watched as he slowly made his way to one spot and started digging. She watched as he tossed and punched and ripped and shred his way down. And then he stopped. She watched in horror as he sat back and raised the skull to start talking to it.

"Jim?" Sheriff Handler said, while stepping into the light with her raised weapon.

"Hello," Jim said without looking up. He then turned and faced the sheriff and raised the skull. "Say hello to my sister, Lucy."

THE END

Illuminator

John and Mary Clarkson had been married for forty-four years now. Both were retired teachers and spent way too much time together. Mary hoped that every day John would find some sort of hobby that would get him out of the house and become more active. Hell, even golf, bowling or fishing down at the docks would be better than just watching television and movies. All he usually did was get in the way trying to help her out around the house.

Mary had left John watching Sports Center when she went down to help out at the church just before noon. She left him a sandwich on the counter, and he knew how to make coffee for himself. Next week was Easter and the fund raiser for food and clothing needed help sorting and cataloging. John waved good-bye when she left without averting his gaze from the sixty-inch screen.

When Mary returned home many hours later, she entered the house through the garage door and saw that the plate was in the sink. Not washed mind you, or in the dish washer, but lying in the sink with a coffee cup and the associated silverware. As she thought that, Mary wondered why they still called it silverware when most of it was crap steel from Wal-Mart. She called to John and received no answer.

Mary tossed her purse onto the kitchen table and pulled the ravioli from the refrigerator to put it in a pot to start boiling. She called John again with the same results. Shaking her head, she opened and started cutting up the sausage that she would put into the sauce. She also diced some onion, garlic and assorted herbs to join the flavored meat.

When the sauce and water were both under way, Mary rinsed her hands and went in search of her husband. The living room television was still on and she could see his head over the top of his recliner. She thought to herself that he must have fallen asleep and not have heard her. She walked around to face him and gasped, then screamed and tried backing away only to trip and fall onto her back. She scrambled and crawled to the phone and dialed nine-one-one.

*　　　　*　　　　*　　　　*

Detective Steve Kruger stood in the living room watching as the Medical Examiner, Doctor Carl Travis, did his thing. They've known each other for a long time and respected each other to a point. Detective Kruger had more respect for the doctor than was reciprocated. The doctor knew all of the stories and thought that the detective was a loose cannon, and more than just a little bit off to the side mentally, but also knew that Kruger more than carried his weight when it came to doing the job.

In front of him was a dead man, sitting in a chair with blinking Christmas lights where his eyes, nose and teeth used to be. The perpetrator had removed the back of the man's head, lifted out the brain, which was now cradled in his own hands, and pressed the lights into position from inside. The missing teeth were scattered around their feet and were being picked up and cataloged by one of the Crime Scene Techs. This was the fourth such case, or similar in the last three months. The perpetrator, or multiple perps, were on a fast schedule, which was out of the norm for most serial offenders.

Detective Steve Kruger was good at what he did. Not only did he get assigned the crazy cases here locally, he was sometimes lent out to the FBI to help catch the really out there serial murderers when the Feds seemed to be at a dead end. He smokes too much, drinks too much, sometimes on the job, which is usually over-looked as long as he doesn't fuck something up. He hasn't done that in a long time. His demeanor and attitude also make him sort of a loner. No-one wants to work with him. He tends to be condescending, nasty and stand-offish.

"Well, Doc," he finally broke the silence. "What the fuck is this guy after?"

"That's your area Detective. What I can tell you is almost the same as we've seen in the other cases. The victim was strangled from the rear, probably with a cord of some sort. His scalp was peeled open from the back to maintain his face, the incision runs along the skull line in a 'U' shaped pattern. His skull was then opened with a bone saw or rotary style tool. I'm leaning toward rotary tool since they are much more easily obtained, but will have that answer shortly after the first few bone analyses come back. The lights are then inserted violently into their final positions."

"What a thing to have done. This ass-hole needs me to find him."

"And you will, Detective, I am sure of it."

"Humph. Why the lights? What do you think it means, psychologically speaking?"

"Not a clue."

They were interrupted when a police officer approached looking for Detective Kruger. "Sir, the woman is about ready to talk. The paramedics think you should come there now."

Detective Kruger nodded and turned to the doctor, "I'll catch up with you later."

The doctor shook his head and continued bagging the dead man's brain. Detective Kruger walked up to the woman sitting up on the gurney outside of the ambulance and introduced himself. After checking her name, address and asking benign questions, meant to see that she was within her faculties, Detective Kruger started with the tougher things. Knowing that she was an elderly lady, Kruger didn't expect too much. He wasn't disappointed. Without issuing any pleasantries or condolences, which would have been the norm, Kruger got to the point where he knew he was wasting his time and just turned and walked away.

*   *   *   *

Detective Kruger was sitting at his desk in the bull pen, as they called it, jotting down notes and thoughts about the latest attack when he heard a voice.

"Detective Kruger? We're from the FBI and we came to offer some help."

Kruger looked up at the two men standing in front of him and said, "The coffee maker is in there, I take it black with two sugars." He then looked back down at his work.

"Not that kind of help," the taller of the two Feds chimed in.

"Then go home."

"We can help with this case. There are things…"

"Look, pal, The FBI calls me in to help with their cases. Do you really think that now I need theirs? If you do…"

"We know who you are."

"…go into that office. You'll find eleven file boxes on top of the table with all the info me and the guys have compiled over the last three months. By the time you guys are up to speed on all the fucking details, that we know forwards and back, we'll already have made the collar."

The taller Fed was about to say something when the Captain walked over. "So glad to see you guys are getting along." He turned to Kruger, "Play nice."

Kruger looked at the Captain, but said to the Feds, "Like I said, the files are in there. Help yourself." He got up and put on his jacket that was hanging from the back of his chair. "When I get back from the Coroner's office, I'll add those notes and findings to the list."

The taller Fed started following Kruger out of the office, "I'll come with. I like to see this shit for myself."

"Suit yourself, but keep quiet. This is my case. When I think I need your help, I'll let you know."

Kruger lit up as soon as he got in the car and the Fed lowered his window. "We really can help. I saw you out in Colorado a few years ago when you helped bring in the 'Mountain Hanger'. Just trying to return the favor. Not looking for more than that."

Kruger just looked at the guy for a moment and then back at the road.

"Agent Thom Buckman, by the way."

In the medical building, they went in through the rear door and down the stairs to the morgue area. They found and put on disposable booties and lab coats. After knocking, the two men went in to find Doctor Travis about halfway through the autopsy. They walked up to the table without saying a word and looked at the man's open chest. The doctor was talking into the headset with his findings.

"…for a seventy-six-year-old. His stomach contents suggest that he had just finished eating a light lunch when he was attacked. The amount of digestion indicates that the food hadn't been in there longer than a few minutes prior to death." The doctor looked up at the two men and nodded. "The good news that I have for you is that it was definitely a rotary type saw with a four-inch cutting blade, probably carbide. The incision on the back of the head is smooth, which leads me to think of a scalpel or a very sharp small bladed knife. His cutting is getting better with the practice. There was less hesitation on this work, than even on the last one. We thought for a moment that we had found a fingerprint on the skull bone, but it is way too smudged and degraded offering no points of recognition."

"Thanks for that Doc," Kruger said. "What about foreign DNA?"

"Nothing so far, it all seems to have come from the vic."

"What are the chances that we will get something useful off of the wire, or sockets, or bulb bases?"

"Slim to none, if they are like the last set. This guy takes great care to not leave us much."

"Any guesses on why the head again? This is the fourth victim and again with the head."

"Your guess is as good as mine Detective, probably better. When you find him, maybe he can answer that for you."

"And Doc, you got anything for a pain in my ass?" Kruger asked tipping his head towards the FBI man standing next to him. He didn't expect or wait for an answer.

*　　　　*　　　　*　　　　*

David watched as the woman made her way into the house. He needed her to shut off the alarm. She never re-set it once inside. That made it a little easier to get in. David finished the cigarette he was smoking and placed the butt in his pocket. He didn't want to leave anything for the investigators. His backpack was heavy and cutting into the tops of his shoulders, so he took a moment to re-adjust them.

Once inside he would have to find the woman and act fast to secure her without too much damage. This time he was going to do his best to leave her alive when he was through with her. Let that cop deal with that for a time.

Elisabeth Neus was tired. She had worked all day, stopped by the store on the way home for something to make for dinner and then swung by her mother's to look in on her. She put water in a pot to heat up for some noodles and poured herself a glass of Frangelica to take the edge off. It might take two or three glasses tonight, but she was prepared. She leaned against the counter's edge and started un-buttoning her blouse to un-hook her bra. She gasped a big sigh of relief right after the clasp was un-done and all the pressure was off.

David watched this happen from outside the window. Smiling to himself, he played with the catch without ever taking his eyes off of the prize. Apparently, Elisabeth had never opened this window and David was finding that the many layers of paint were retarding his progress. The woman turned away and left the room. He worked faster prying against the latex barrier. Feeling it finally give way and allowing the window to rise. He hoisted himself up with no effort and slid the panel closed behind him. David knew that the woman would be back in this room soon, so he stood still against the wall and waited. He could do that all night.

Closing down external stimuli was easy for David. He found that out during the many beatings he received as a child from his mother. David's father had died when he was young, and his mother never got over it. Constantly complaining about David being in the way of her happiness and why she wasn't finding someone else. So, the beatings went on and on. David learned that when he turned inward, the pain and screaming went away. So, he retreated to a world that no others had access to. This trait even helped at work when meetings would last all morning and some of the attendees would nod off, David was refreshed by the internal oasis. That would be Christmas morning when he was five years old and the whole family had been happy.

Footsteps brought David back to the moment. The footsteps were getting closer, so he prepared. Elisabeth stepped into the room and saw a man swinging his hand at her face. She had no time to react, basically walking right into the blow. Snapping nasal cartilage and splattering blood followed Elisabeth as she collapsed to the Spanish tile floor. With her head spinning she was no match for the next blow which sent her into deep sleep.

Excruciating pain brought Elisabeth back to Hell. She was tightly secured in a spread-eagle position on her bed and cold from the lack of clothing. There was fire on her right side and Elisabeth, still reeling turned in that direction to see a man. The man had his hand inside of her. Her eyes and mind couldn't understand what she was seeing. The man's hand was under her skin pressing something hard against the inside of her nipple. She watched as her nipple pressed up and stretched before ripping away to allow the bright red Christmas tree light to emerge. Elisabeth tried to scream, but only managed a slight airy exhale before passing out again.

*　　　　*　　　　*　　　　*

Even Detective Kruger was appalled by what he was watching. The paramedics were trying to keep the poor woman alive while the investigators took pictures. The mad man had placed a light bulb through each nipple, one was popping out of her belly button, and apparently the remaining seven were bunched tightly protruding from her vaginal opening. Most of the wiring was subcutaneous, or under the skin. He had made slits along Elisabeth's sides and forced his hands between the skin and muscle layer, much like the nozzle on a liposuction device. The damage physically was minimal all things considered, but the pain would have been unbearable.

Detective Kruger and his team would have to wait until the morning to even consider questioning the woman. The pain relievers would have her out of it at least that long. The Crime Scene Technician, who took the pictures from every conceivable angle, downloaded a set onto his laptop before handing Detective Kruger a thumb drive with his own set to review. Kruger lit up a cigarette as the ambulance pulled away from the curb.

"Hell of a thing to see first thing in the morning."

Kruger turned to see Agent Thom Buckman standing there. "I didn't see you inside."

"I wasn't. I talked to the first responding police officer. He is past the point of throwing up now." The last was added with a knowing smirk.

Kruger wanted to hit the guy but knew that that was not the thing to do just now. "Yeah, well, we all have bad days."

"This guy is speeding up, Detective."

"Yeah, but this time we can at least find out what the fucker looks like."

"Did she let him in?" the Fed asked.

"No, he opened a window on the side of the house. All we know right now is that he was wearing size eleven shoes when he did."

"So, he's a tall guy."

Kruger shook his head. "Only if you assume that he was wearing shoes that fit his feet, and not a few pairs of socks and bigger shoes as a red hearing."

The FBI guy nodded his understanding.

"There were also fresh cigarette ashes lying at the base of a tree along the yards back edge. The guy's a smoker. In the morning we'll know which brand."

Kruger pinched off the top of his cigarette and dropped the butt in his own pocket. "I'll get the pics up first thing when I get back, in case you're interested in seeing them." He opened his door and climbed into the old county issued unmarked vehicle. Without looking back, he started the engine and pulled off leaving the FBI man standing there on the sidewalk.

It was almost midnight when Detective Kruger called it a day and walked the two blocks to the pub, he was a regular at. He walked in and the waitress poured his drink even before his ass hit the stool. She winked at him and went about her business. Seven drinks and four hours later, Detective Kruger said good night to the waitress as she closed up shop. He made his way, a little less sure on his feet, back to his car. He crawled into the rear seat and promptly went to sleep against his curled-up overcoat.

*   *   *   *

Neither the cars entering and leaving the lot, nor the light, stirred Detective Kruger, but the knock on the car's window did. He looked up to see Agent Buckman standing there holding a cup of coffee. He spun around and opened the door.

"Good morning to you too," Kruger offered.

"It's good to see you here almost on time, Detective."

"Fuck you," Kruger said as he sipped the coffee, "was here until midnight."

"I know and closed the local bar at four."

"You following me?"

"Well, we are working together, right?"

Kruger climbed from the car and the two men went to the office. Two other day detectives were there. Kruger told them that the pics and test results were up from yesterday. As he reviewed the info with the Fed and drank his coffee, his phone rang.

"Kruger…yeah…very nice…we'll be right over, twenty minutes…see ya." He sat back and sipped his coffee. "She's awake and talking. I guess you can come with me," he said to the Fed, toasting him with the coffee cup. Agent Buckman followed Kruger to the Captain's office where Kruger explained what they knew and where they were going.

*   *   *   *

"Hello, Elisabeth, my name is Steve Kruger and I am the Detective on your case. This is Agent Buckman, from the FBI." He let that sink in. "I know you went over this with the police officers, but we really need you to tell us in your own words what happened."

For the next hour, with small breaks for water and rest, Elisabeth went over it again and again. The pain she relived was terrible, even to hear this way. They now had a picture of this guy. One they could go after. They thanked her for all of her help and walked away in search of coffee and a space to write. The doctor had already supplied them with all the things that he could. Her injuries, though painful and horrific, she would recover from. There would be scaring, she had lost her left nipple, and the openings had been rough and torn and were going to leave larger scars.

"How can people go around all day not knowing what is going on around them?" the Fed asked Kruger.

"They don't want to know, until they need us. Then it's 'Where were you?'"

"That paints a pretty sad picture there, Steve."

"It's why we have jobs." Kruger lit up as soon as they were outside of the door. "Without the bad guys and ignorance, we'd be selling used cars."

*   *   *   *

Dave bound the couple face to face. They were still alive, but not struggling. Fear and pain had them somewhat subdued. The lights draped around their necks brightened the bedroom and Dave's mood. The woman who was definitely in her late forties, was still pretty hot and Dave considered doing other things with her, but rape wasn't his thing and he wasn't getting aroused enough.

"Who would like to be first?" Dave asked while pointing the knife back and forth between them like 'eeny-meeny-miney-moe'. "Keep in mind it won't be easy for either party."

The woman said, "Kill me first, you son-of-a-bitch."

The husband's head snapped up to look at her in the eye. "Honey?"

"You're stronger. When he's distracted with me you can get out and take care of him. Right?"

He understood what she was saying and doing. "Of course. Love ya."

"Love you too." Then she turned towards their captor. "Do it, you fuck."

Dave stepped alongside the woman, reached across and slit the husband's throat. The pulsing blood shot into her face and she screamed like nothing Dave had ever heard, and he had heard a lot. The shock in the man's eyes faded to fear and then slowly to acceptance as the blood continued to pump. The light in those eyes didn't last much after the blood flow had became a trickle. The woman's screams turned to sobbing with the occasional 'fuck you' tossed in between gasping breaths.

Dave petted the woman's hair, "Thank you for your courage."

"Fuck you."

She was forced to watch as Dave mutilated her husband. After coming to, having passed out, she felt

Dave's hands on her neck and knew the end was coming, wishing for it to be fast and painless, but knowing it wouldn't be so. The blade felt like a tickle and then a rush of pain. Watching her own blood soaking her dead husband drove her crazy in those last moments before she died. Her attempts at screaming only caused the blood to spray from the severed larynx, never reaching the animated, silent mouth.

*   *   *   *

Detective Kruger stood with the Medical Examiner as the doctor went over the preliminary cause of death. The couple was found this morning, but had died more than two nights ago. Each had had their throats slashed open and the lights had been inserted through their mouths to protrude out the new opening. Each of the victims had five lights blinking on and off. The dried, blackened blood cast eerie shadows on the walls and faces of the victims. There wasn't much for the doctor to tell them. The loss of blood is what had killed them. The mutilation was done after death. He couldn't determine how long it had been between the deaths to tell if one had witnessed the other's maiming.

When Detective Kruger returned to the office later in the day. He had planned on just dropping off the latest info to be entered into the system and head out, but one of the Feds was there waiting for him.

"What happened out there?"

"He killed a couple this time," Kruger answered while continuing to walk past the man.

"Anything we can do?"

"Yeah, go do whatever it is you guys do. Find something to canvas." The closing of the door cut off the other answer and brought an ever so slight smirk to Kruger's face. He walked to his thinking bar, grabbed a small booth along the window and ordered two drinks and a burger with fries. He sat there all day looking at maps and locations. He knew he was missing something but knew he would find it here. When there was nothing except greasy remains on the plate and a fourth empty glass on the table, a shadow encroached his space. It was the Agent Buckman. "Still following me, huh?"

"I knew I would find you here. It's your favorite hang out." He nodded to the waitress and pointed to the glasses holding two fingers raised.

"I didn't want to intrude…"

"Like now?"

"…but wanted to see how you're getting on. I talked to the Coroner. This is one fucked up guy we're hunting.

"Got that right."

"Why the maps? Looking for a geographical component to all of this?"

"Answering your own question. My tax dollars at work."

"You always such a prick?"

"You came to me, pal. Deal with it."

The Fed sat back with his drink and took a big gulp. "Fair enough." His eyes never left Steve's. "So, now with the pleasantries out of the way. Mind telling me what you found?"

Steve lit up and pushed the map towards the Fed. "I circled the sites in red. Notice anything peculiar?"

The Fed took his time studying the picture in front of him. Steve sat back and puffed smoke rings up towards the ceiling between sips from his glass. Finally, Agent Buckman looked up. "What am I missing?"

"Familiarity with the area and things local."

"Subtle nuances an outsider wouldn't catch, you mean."

"Exactly. It took me a while to see it too. Each location is within three blocks of a bus drop off point. You know those little kiosks you see on the streets?"

"Yeah. Same bus?"

"Got someone checking on that for me now. Waiting for the call."

The Fed nodded in appreciation of the find. "Think he's a driver, or a rider?"

"Rider. This bastard has too much time on his hand to be driving a bus all over the city. How could he follow the vics?"

"They took the bus too?"

"Recently, yeah. Every one of them. Broken down cars, missed a carpool, etcetera."

"And that was in your reports?"

"Nope. Made calls after I saw the pattern. I was right."

"Then we got him."

"Maybe," Kruger said while lighting another cigarette, "he'll be on watch for someone like us. Gonna have to use a decoy, and that could take time."

*   *   *   *

Dave got off the bus at the next block and quickly walked back to catch up with the woman. He'd seen her the last few days and dreamt about what he would do to her last night. He hoped that he would spot her again today. He did. After the brisk walk, he re-adjusted the backpack and slowed to keep within viewing distance of his prey. He knew where she lived. He had followed her last night. She was new to the neighborhood and without a car. He figured that she must have been recently divorced or something. A piece of ass like her wouldn't be single long, not around here.

Cathy Maio walked at her regular pace and listened to the earpiece. Detective Kruger had known her from Vice and had gotten permission to borrow her for a while. She was perfect. Not too old, or young, with decent looks. She would catch this guys eyes. He knew it.

"There's a guy coming up fast."

"I got him. He's slowing to keep pace."

"Just be cool Cat, act natural."

When she got to the door, she made the effort of setting her packages down before fumbling with her keys. After opening the door, she left it open and came out to get the packages. She didn't see anyone and went back inside.

"He's going to the back. Who's got eyes?"

Cathy Maio put the packages on the kitchen table and backed to the living room, sat on the couch and placed her pistol between the cushions. This waiting was natural to her. Many a night was spent in some seedy motel when Johns were no shows. You can get used to a lot.

"There's movement by the back door. He's low and working the lock."

"Be cool Cat, I'm right with you. Blake and Edwards move closer on foot. No cars or lights or nothing to spook this guy."

"Got it," came over the radio twice.

"He's in."

Sergeant Maio tensed a bit when she heard that, but quickly fought off those feelings. She had to be ready. She stood up, turned on the light and started taking off her shoes, kicking them to the side. Then she started with the tee shirt. She was wearing a sports bra under it so wouldn't be embarrassed when her 'rescuers' came through the door.

"We're right outside the front door. Code word and we're in."

Cathy didn't even hear the guy when he came into the room. He had taken his shoes off outside and was only wearing his socks. When she turned, he was standing right there with a fist swinging towards her face.

"RED, RED, RED!"

She half blocked the punch, feeling her head being smacked to the side. The front door and bedroom doors both flew open and six men rushed into the room with raised weapons. The shocked killer leapt over the couch and landed a perfect head kick to the shorter of the two Feds. By then, he was swarmed and tossed roughly to the carpeted floor. For a moment, Kruger had wished that it had been hard wood or tile instead.

Cuffed and hog tied, the man was lifted to sit on the couch. He was read his rights and had his backpack examined. Everything the men had figured that they would find was there. Knives, rope, wire, and three strings of Christmas lights.

Detective Kruger lifted the guys chin to look him dead in the eyes. "Turn out the lights, the party's over." A few laughs and smiles filled the room.

THE END

Bad Ink

Detective Tom Reingold was having a hard time believing the stories that he was hearing. He was on a murder case that seemingly had no motive, no witnesses and no suspects. All that he had was a dead guy with his own arm, or parts of it, in his stomach. The Medical Examiner, or ME, wasn't even sure how the parts had gotten in there. He had told the detective that it looked as if they had been bitten off and swallowed. When pressed further, the doctor had no explanation.

*   *   *   *

The poor guy was sitting at his kitchen table, well, slumped down over it now, with his left arm a bloody stump. There were large brutal gashes and possibly teeth marks in the surrounding tissues. The remains of the humorous bone stuck out grey and pink, the end having been snapped off. The man's head lie on the table at an angle where his dry, grey eyes could stare unblinkingly at the stump. The silence in the room was being broken by the syncopated dripping of the blood off of the table's edge onto the wooden floor.

The blood had pooled under the arm, or what was left of it, on the table and was inching towards the edge as well as to the man's face where it followed the outline along the surface. Arterial spray had gotten the side wall and the cabinets were soaked with blood. Bloody crooked lines and splatter covered most of their surfaces.

Tom asked the doctor, "Hey, Doc, do you think his head was turned that way after he was dead, or did he die watching what was happening to him?"

"No way to know, Tom."

"Fuck, man. I wouldn't want to watch my arm being eaten," his partner added.

Along with everything else, there were blood droplets and smears on the dead guys back, right next to a very realistic looking tattoo of the head of a T-Rex, the bad-ass dinosaur, with a human lying below without an arm. Of course, the speculation around the club house was that the dino had done it. Tom was feeling the pressure and the ribbing was starting to get to him.

The victim, a Greg Thomas, hadn't shown up for work this morning and a friend stopped by after work to see if he was okay. Finding Greg's car in the parking lot and getting no response at the door or phone, she called the police. That was how he was found, and the female friend was still in the emergency room, having passed out and hitting her head on the door frame after seeing the death. His boss and co-workers all agreed that Greg, though a little strange, was a good guy. He didn't do drugs, but engaged in social drinking, and had only a few close friends, an ex-girlfriend and an ex-boyfriend. The guy's apartment looked like a typical single guy's lair. There were girly and gay mags, a lot of takeout containers in the garbage bin. There was limited food in the refrigerator and freezer, some of which was way beyond its expiration date.

Tom and his partner, Detective Frank Willis, walked around the apartment. They had spoken to his landlord, who swore that Greg was a model tenant. He had always paid his rent on time and offered to do little fixes himself. They had found little to suggest that Greg had been into anything devious. There were tattoo magazines and pictures on the wall, so the detectives thought that they should look into when and where Greg had gotten the dinosaur.

*　　　　*　　　　*　　　　*

Detective Tom Reingold entered the tattoo parlor, or shop, as they are now referred to. Along the walls were stencils of a wide variety of tattoo designs from butterflies to skulls and knives. There were also pictures of completed tattoos and piercings. Tom took a moment to look at a few that he found unbelievable and shocking. Why would anyone in their right mind have their genitals pierced with large metal devices? Or for that matter bury spikes in their head and cheeks? Tom just didn't get it, and he was sure that it was more than an age thing, though at forty-two, he didn't consider himself old. The slightly over-weight woman behind the counter could have easily posed for some of the pictures in the shop. She had tattoos on most of her exposed skin and had ear, nose, eyebrow, lip and tongue piercings. Tom was certain that there could be other piercings, but he really didn't need to know about them or care enough to find out. Tom was thinking that the woman might have been cute had she not done this to herself.

"How can I help you, sweetie?" the woman asked as Tom approached the counter.

The counter was mostly glass and contained metal pieces that apparently went into all sorts of body parts. Tom flashed his shield and said, "I'm Detective Tom Reingold and I need to talk to the proprietor about a person who we believe got their tattoos here."

The woman nodded and said, "There are certain confidentially things in place and I'm not sure we can discuss our clients."

"Even dead ones?"

That brought the woman's complaints to a sudden halt. "Uh…dead?"

Tom pulled out his cell phone and pulled up a small photograph of the victim and hoped that he had been here. The woman looked it over. "Yeah, he's been here, but not in a long time."

"Well, the Coroner says that his most recent tattoo, a T-Rex, is about a month old."

"He didn't get it here."

"If I showed you the tattoo could you possibly recognize the artist?"

"I could try, Hon, but I won't promise. There are way too many shops poppin' up with nobodies, you know?"

Tom showed her the tattoo. The woman shook her head no and then called over her shoulder to the back area that was separated by a beaded curtain for a Dusty to come up. Dusty was an older, world weary looking individual very covered in old and new tattoos. He looked at the tattoo picture and looked Tom in the eye. "Yeah, I know about this guy, but you don't want no part of him."

"Why's that?"

"He's like scary bad. Voodoo and bullshit, like a head case. Too many blows to the head as a kid or too much drugs or something."

"You know where to find this…head case?"

"He don't have like a place like this. He's all like underground or word of mouth shit. Try over in the campgrounds."

The campgrounds were an area off of South Fifteenth Street where the homeless had set up and taken over. It was made up of tents, lean-tos and all sorts of other makeshift temporary 'homes'. At any given time there were between four and five hundred un-documented individuals living there.

"You think this guy could be a killer?"

"Yo man, I ain't that deep into his stuff. Know what I mean?"

"Okay, I hear you. Do you have a name?"

"Only thing I know him by is, and I hope I pronounce it right for you, Samedi."

"Samedi?" Tom asked for clarification.

"Yeah, Samedi. The Voodoo devil or something."

*   *   *   *

Detective Tom Reingold was sitting in the diner going over his notes when his partner Detective Frank Willis plopped down opposite him. Frank waved to the waitress and she was soon at the table taking his order. A double bacon cheeseburger, fries, onion rings, cheesecake and a large Pepsi, not Coke. Tom looked at him and shook his head. "Guess I should start looking for a new partner if you keep eating shit like that, Frank."

"Don't worry about me, Tom. When you're long gone, I'll be still eating and looking this good." That got a laugh out of both of them and the waitress. "Anyway, get a load of this…" he glanced at the waitress, who took the cue and moved on. "…Apparently, this isn't the first weird case like this. When I called a buddy over in the Tenth, he told me that they had a case there. Not like exactly the same, but weird with no witnesses, no motive or reason. Just a dead vic in bad condition. When I asked him about the tattoo angle, he said he would look into it and get back to me. I asked if he ever heard of a Samedi character he said, yeah, but only rumors. Nobody's apparently got a line on this guy."

Between bites of his turkey club, Tom said, "Maybe we'll have some luck over in the campgrounds. I'm sort of friendly with a few regulars there."

"I hate that place, it gives me the creeps."

"Yeah, but it's just the sort of place a guy like this killer would hide out. Out in the open, so to speak, and surround with people too afraid to ask questions or to turn him in."

"Yeah," Frank said, "but the same could be said of most of the strip clubs and biker bars."

"I suppose, but..." Tom took a big bite, "bikers are a tough crowd and this guy is going after softer targets. Also, so far this guy hasn't killed a woman."

The waitress interrupted the conversation when she brought Frank's loaded plates to the table. For the next fifteen minutes, Tom watched, almost in awe, as Frank polished off the double burger, the fries and onion rings and then the cake. There was little conversation until Frank sat back from the table with an audible belch. "Much better," he smiled. Tom shook his head. He sat back sipping his coffee when his phone rang.

"Reingold...yeah...hold on a sec," he pulled out his pad and a pen to take notes. It was Martin Gold, the ME. "Okay, shoot...uh-huh...yeah...no way...Christ...okay, Doc, thanks for the update...Tomorrow morning would be great...see ya."

Detective Frank Willis was drinking his coffee and picking his teeth while waiting for the conversation to end. "What do we know?"

Tom looked at him, "This is fucked up. Our Mr. Thomas had almost his entire arm in his stomach. Doc Martin says that it looks like it was shoved down his throat in pieces. The esophagus, larynx and surrounding tissue is all but completely destroyed. The parts were roughly smashed into the man tearing his shit apart as it went down."

"Damn. That would have taken time and strength."

"Yeah, and it also means that he was dead before, or died with the first assault."

"What a way to go, I don't even want to think like that."

"Yeah," Tom said. He gulped the remains of his coffee and nodded for them to leave.

After paying the check, the two men their way through the afternoon traffic to the campgrounds. Sadly, a lot of the people recognized the police when they saw them and moved away quickly, acted dumb or tried to hide. Tom understood that being down on your luck and homeless wasn't a good place to be, but to be afraid of the good guys seemed like a bad idea to him. Yeah, there were bad cops, just like there are bad people, who would abuse the trust of the downtrodden, but still, the majority of them were there to serve and protect. Over the last nine or ten years, a few cases had brought Tom to the campgrounds and during those times he had made a few good contacts that were always willing to give him some good information, for a price. The problem was in finding them. Being nomadic and living in an ever-changing environment made even the long timers hard to find.

Tom stopped to light a cigarette and Frank shook his head. "Sure, the bacon is bad for me, but he lights up. What an unfair world we live in." Tom puffed the smoke in his direction.

"Yo, Mister Tom."

The detectives turned to see Jimmy 'The Head' coming their way. He was called that out of respect. Tom thought for sure that the man had the largest head in the world and was surprised that he could even walk without falling over. The rest of his body was average sized for a man living on the street for the last, well, forever Tom would have guessed. His head though looked like a bobble head caricature.

"Hey, Jimmy. How's it going?"

"You know, like the same thing every day."

Tom offered the man a cigarette and Jimmy greedily snatched three or four, stuffing all but one into his pocket. After lighting the one in his hand, Jimmy asked, "So what brings you fine gentlemen down this end of town?"

"We're looking for some information on a guy that might have been through here. He's a pretty bad guy and we would like to find him and stop him before he hurts any more people."

"Sounds reasonable," he let the silence fill the void and then asked, "So who is it?"

"He calls himself Samedi," he paused to let that sink in, then added, "and he might be involved with tattooing or voodoo."

"I ain't never heard that name around here."

"You sure?"

"Yeah, I woulda remembered that."

"What about underground tattoo artists?"

"They all over, but they usually have to squat in some building to have the electricity, you know? Did you look over on Twelfth by the car guys?"

"Why? You hearing things about over there?"

"You asked about tattoos, I'd look over there." He pointed off to the detective's left. The two detectives looked where he was pointing and when Tom looked back, Jimmy was moving off, scuffling along and looking at the cigarette he was holding as if it had just appeared there. Jimmy had been pointing to an old beat up camper-trailer looking thing, so the detectives headed in that direction. The sign said 'Tattoo', but what they found was an old man with little to no equipment who showed them pictures that weren't even in the same league as what they were looking for. He also didn't know anything or anyone who could have done the ones in the photos.

As they were making their way back to the car, Detective Frank Willis said, "Great, another dead end."

Tom answered, "Maybe not, Jimmy said something about tattoos being done over by all the car chop shops. It might be worth checking out. We can put in a call to vice and see what they know."

*   *   *   *

II

The following afternoon, Detective Tom Reingold and Detective Frank Willis were standing in another apartment with another dead body and a lot of crime scene techs. They were waiting on the Medical Examiner to get there to give them the un-official official findings. What the two detectives could see though bothered them. The man's naked body was lying across the living room floor, and at his neck was a big puddle of dried, coagulated blood. Flies were in and out of it despite the activity in the room. The body was slightly bloated from the decomposition gasses building up inside of it, the stretching skin turning purple and black. The man's head had rolled a foot or so from the body and was staring across the room towards the door. Matthew Franklin wouldn't be answering it any time soon.

The head had been neatly severed by an apparently very sharp object. That wasn't what had the detectives upset, as each had witnessed this sort of thing, or worse, before. What had gotten them called in and involved in this case was the very large detailed back-piece tattoo. It depicted a guillotine with a bloody, dropped blade. You could see part of the body on the far side of the blade, and the man's severed head was lying in the foreground. The face could have been a photograph of the present victim. The tattoo artist had captured Matthew's fate in his art, or as Tom was thinking and suggesting, maybe the other way around.

Detective Reingold asked one of the technicians with the camera to print him out very clear shots of the tattoo. He also asked the room, "Do any of you guys have tattoos?"

One of the younger techs approached him, "I do."

Tom asked the man, "How long would it take to tattoo something this big and detailed?"

"Oh, wow. It would probably be a few sittings of five to six hours each. That's a lot of work."

Detective Willis followed up with, "So, he probably didn't do it after the guy was dead?"

"Oh, no way. This is healed and done maybe a few months ago. This isn't new."

The two detectives thanked him for his input and stepped outside so that Tom could light up. "What the hell is going on, Frank?"

"Someone had to have set this up. Either they knew about the tattoo previously, or they gave it to him and came back to make it real."

"I'm thinking that we need to get a line on this Samedi guy."

"You ain't buying into all that voodoo talk are you, Tom?"

"No, but I do have a feeling that he is part of what's going on. Killer or not, we need to talk to him…and sooner rather than later."

When the ME arrived, he was just as perplexed as the detectives were. He looked long and hard at the neck trauma before shaking his head. "If I didn't know better, I'd say the machine on his back did this. The cut is very clean and quite possibly done in one fluid motion."

"Could something like a samurai sword have done this?" Tom asked.

"I've heard that you could decapitate with one, but I personally have never seen the results. You should probably find a samurai instructor or Kendo school to ask that of them."

"Kendo?"

"Yeah, I'm sure there are some around, use the internet."

"Thanks," Tom wrote a few things down and then asked, "What about a time of death?"

"Looking at what I see here, I would guess somewhere between seventy-two and ninety hours."

"So, before the other guy?"

"I would say so, yeah." The doc walked around the victim, "Another interesting tattoo angle, huh, Tom?"

"You got that right. And I'm guessing it didn't do this?" He asked with a smile and a wink.

The ME leaned closer to the dead man's back and using an evidence swab, rubbed the bottom of the inked blade. The swab came away covered in semi-dried blood. "Maybe you can't discount that, guys."

"Just what we need, a killer with a twisted sense of humor."

*　　　　*　　　　*　　　　*

Detective Reingold dropped into the booth across from his partner Detective Willis. The latter was sitting behind two plates of very greasy remnants. "Damn, Frank, isn't that like going to go right through you? All that grease and fat?"

"Tom, this" he said while pointing to himself, "is a finely tuned body and it can handle anything I put into it. I've trained it oh so well." Even the waitress had to laugh at that one.

Tom ordered a chicken Caesar salad, dressing on the side, a baked potato and the bottomless coffee pot.

Without looking up Frank asked, "So, what did the karate guy have to say?"

"He said that it was possible, given the proper blade, a lot of training and practice…"

"How do you practice severing heads?"

"…so, we can't rule out that possibility."

"Back to square fucking one again. I'm getting tired of all this one step forward and a mile back shit."

"Yeah, even I'm getting fed up with this case, and the lack of direction." Tom was about to add to that, but the waitress showed up with his food and he set the folder aside to begin eating. The coffee was hot, and he added just a touch of milk and sugar.

Frank finished mopping his plate with the bread, shoving the last dripping piece into his mouth and sucking his fingers. He sat back and picked up his coffee. "You know, we could be looking at this all wrong."

"How so?"

"What if this is just some nut job, looking for people with crazy tattoos? Maybe he's offended by them?"

"Offended by a tattoo? I find that hard to believe given that fact that both of our guys had them on their backs and probably not seen much by outsiders, except maybe at the beach or public showers, like at the gym."

"Okay, so let's just say that this guy saw them somehow and decided to take out his frustration on the wearer of said tattoo. Followed them home and did the deed."

Tom chewed his mouthful of salad before commenting. "I don't think so. This looks too set up…"

"Exactly, this guy would be stalking them."

"…That would mean a lot of time. I'm thinking that the killer already knew not only what the tattoo was, but where to find the guy. He just shows up and whack…it's done."

Frank grabbed his note pad, "That reminds me. The ME found no other reason for the death of our second victim, Matthew Franklin. No other marks, wounds, etcetera. It appears that the decapitation was quick, and it was the only visible cause of death. He'll have a tox screen back tonight."

"That would lead us back to the sword idea…"

"Or the guillotine."

"…On his back?" Tom almost choked on his food while trying not to laugh.

Frank looked at him seriously. "What if he wasn't killed there, but dumped there?"

"You mean like killed by a guillotine someplace else and then carried up to his apartment like that?" He sat back. "Collect as much blood as possible when it is done and just pour it out at the disposal scene. We should find out from Doc Gold is that was possible from what he saw." He leaned forward onto his elbows, "That ain't bad."

When the two detectives had finished eating, they headed back to the station to look for their Captain. Captain Jason Oliver had served in the military during the gulf wars and had been a cop ever since returning home. He had gotten wounded, but had fully recovered from those physical injuries. The open wounds, if you could call them that, were inside. The loss of his friends and fellow soldiers, it turns out, had left a more permanent mark. He still held a grudge against the terrorists and anyone who harbored and abetted them. He would prefer killing them all to stop the violence and worry about the aftermath when peace was at hand.

They knocked on his door. Captain Oliver was on the phone but waved the two men in and indicated that they could sit. The detectives did and each got their notes out and ready. After setting the phone down and writing a few notes in his log, Captain Oliver looked up, "I hear you guys got another one yesterday."

After a few minutes bringing the captain up to speed on their investigation, Tom said, "We're spinning our wheels here, Captain. Every time we turn around, the leads that seemed promising dry up and blow away. We got nothing. Nothing solid anyway."

"Tell me what you do have."

They did. They even mentioned the sword angle and the possibility that it was a body drop after a real beheading. The first guy with a stomach full of his own arm, still had them guessing. The only real connection could be this elusive Samedi guy and the tattoos.

Captain Oliver sat back and digested what he was told. "I'd follow up the tattoo angle. Somebody gave them those tats and everything else seems to be all about them. The large bites and digested arm, and this beheading." He leaned forward to rest on his desk using his elbows, "That is sort of creepy that guy having his own face back there." His body shook for a moment to ward off the chill creeping up his arms. He sipped his coffee and grimaced as the cold bitter fluid hit his tongue, "Beat the bushes. Hit all of the tattoo joints and find out who did them. Or maybe who they think might have. Get something, and find this Samedi guy."

The two detectives left him with that and headed out into the night.

*　　　　　*　　　　　*　　　　　*

It was late in the afternoon and the sun was starting to set when the two detectives decided to stop to eat. They had been at it since they had left the office almost nine hours ago. "Damn, Tom, just how many more of these places are on the list?"

"Shit, we're barely halfway through it." Tom laughed.

"Shit is right."

Over a few burgers at the local Irish pub, they went over what they had learned. They found out over the course of the day that there were a lot of crazy people out there getting tattoos of almost anything that the mind can imagine, and that the artist could sketch up. They also learned way more about body piercing than either had ever wanted to know. Three of the twenty-two places that they had been too had heard of this Samedi guy, and they strongly urged the detectives to stay clear of him. There were eleven places left to hit

As they ate, Detective Willis, received a phone call. "Willis …okay…oh really?...give me that address again." He flipped open the notebook and started writing. "Hey, thanks Gloria, that's a big help." After hanging up the phone he turned to Tom. "Gloria got us a line on a local religious professional who apparently knows a ton of stuff about voodoo and other occult type things. We'll see if he can tell us what this guy is all about and what he should look like. Even the tattoo guys, who've said that they've heard of him, can't give us a description worth doing anything with."

"That's good, another angle to follow up on. Maybe we'll finally get a picture of what this ghost looks like."

"Great," Frank chimed in sarcastically, "more craziness to end the day on."

When they finished eating, they split up. Frank would hit the last of the tattoo places while Tom went to see this religious man and get the scoop on the Samedi character. They would meet back at the office when each was through.

*　　　　*　　　　*　　　　*

Detective Reingold was almost done with his reports for the day, when his partner showed up. Frank walked over saying, "I never want to see that again."

"What did you see?"

"In the second to last place, there was a woman getting her, get this, vaginal lips pierced. She was having something like forty little metallic hoops installed, is installed the right word? And then a fancy ribbon was being passed through them to sort of tie it shut. Gave me the fucking willies."

"Yeah, I don't think I would want to see that either. What did you find out?"

"Well, two more places had heard of the guy and mentioned that he was a loose cannon, a little crazy and very dangerous. One thinks he is down in the campgrounds, just like we'd heard the other day. They both said that he might be taller than average, a light black-skinned male, and one guy said that he wore very old, way out of date clothing. Something from the past, like what our grandfathers used to wear or something." He dropped into his chair, sipped some of the coffee he had been carrying and then asked. "What about you?"

"Well this Samedi character, or Baron Samedi in some circles, is definitely a voodoo God-like guy. He's very disruptive, and yes, very dangerous. That said, he is also the God of…" Tom flipped through his notes, "…resurrection, like bringing people back to life…"

"You talking zombies?"

"…and something about he's always surrounded by whiskey and cigars. Likes the color purple and wears a…top hat."

"You don't see many of those walking around here." Frank said, stating the obvious. "So, it looks like we'll be hitting the grounds again in the morning.

Maybe we'll find someone more talkative before they've had their morning coffee or fix."

*   *   *   *

III

The two detectives got out of the car on the south side of the campgrounds and walked toward the center of the area. They were sweeping for faces that they recognized, looking for someone who might be willing to talk to them and pass on some information for a few dollars and a smoke. Tom was hoping to run into Jimmy 'The Head' again and push him a little bit about the location for the underground tattoo shops. They stopped a few of the people who looked normal enough, but got very little out of them.

After a few more minutes of striking out, Tom saw Jimmy. He was lying on his side, near a wall. The two detectives went over to him. Jimmy 'The Head' had been beaten up. His face was all bruised and his lip was split, and Tom was pretty sure that the nose was going to mend in that twisted broken way unless Jimmy got to the hospital, but he refused to go when Tom mentioned it.

"What happened?" Detective Willis asked the man.

"Man, three guys like heard about me talking to you about this Sam…e…kinda…guy, or what-ever-the-fuck. Got me busted up for it. You should go."

"Jimmy, you know me. Who was it?"

"Just three guys. Light skinned black or island dudes." He sat up and leaned against the wall. "You got any more smokes?"

Tom fished a half-full pack out of his pocket and handed it to the man, he felt it was the least that he could do for him. "Go on."

"Nothin' to tell. They came up on me. Told me that they be hearin' shit and beat me."

"I'm sorry, Jimmy…"

"It ain't your fault, Man. But I think they stay somewhere on the other side."

"In the grounds here?"

"Yeah."

"Would you show us the area?"

"Fuck no. Man, talking to you now is like taking a risk. I think you should be like moseying." He lit one of the cigarettes and Tom watched the sleight of hand as the pack seemed to just disappear into the man's chest. Jimmy 'The Head', pushed up from the wall and limped away towards the coffee truck on the other side of the street.

Detective Willis said, "Man, that's fucked up. He got beat like that because he talked to us."

"Yeah, well…" Tom thought for a moment, "We'll make it up to him by catching the mother-fuckers."

"Let's do it," Frank said. The two detectives started moving deeper into the unpatrolled lawless area of the campgrounds. "Shit, we should have brought backup."

More and more of the inhabitants shied away from them. Closing flaps or what passed for doors to keep them out.

"Hey, you don't belong here."

The two detectives turned as one and found themselves facing three medium sized rough looking characters. As Jimmy had told them, they looked to be either light skinned black men or men from a Caribbean island.

Tom pulled his badge out, "We're here investigating a murder. We've been led here and will go as soon as we have what we came for."

The three men spaced themselves apart as if getting ready for a fight. "You go now," the man in the middle said.

"We'll go when we're good and ready," Tom said, placing his badge back in his jacket and standing firm and erect. "Are you the guys that put the beat down on poor Jimmy?"

The tough guy's eyes flared, but he remained quiet. Staring at Tom eye to eye like two bulls waiting for the other to blink.

Tom continued, "It must make you feel so proud to be part of a team...well to be needing a team to beat up some poor old rundown homeless man. Real big of you."

"Hey, fuck you. You don't live here. You don't know what goes on...at night."

"I know a scum bag when I see one." Turning to Frank he said, "Let's go, these guys don't know anything."

When they turned to leave, Tom heard the audible snap of a baton and spun back with his gun drawn. The man to his left was almost on him, bringing the club down towards Tom's head. Tom fired his service weapon into the man's chest, causing the attacker to stagger back and fall lifeless to the ground. Tom spun to face the leader again. Frank had his weapon out and was drawing a bead on the third man on the right.

"Now, see what you've done? You just got a whole squad coming here now. You couldn't keep this little piece of shit on a leash. You wanted us gone? Because of this, we're going to be up your ass all day now, asshole. On the fucking ground."

The words were barely out of his mouth when the two men turned as one and ran through the gathering crowd.

"Shit," Tom knelt to feel for a pulse on the man that he shot, and not getting one said, "Frank, call it in."

Frank did so while keeping his eyes on the two men pushing away through the gawkers. He noticed which direction that they were moving on and guessed their final destination. There, standing in the distance, was the man that Frank was sure was the one that they were looking for. He was taller than the others, but looked skinny from this far away. He was dressed in an older style overcoat and a top hat. "Tom, ten-o'clock and out about forty yards."

Tom stood up and saw the target right away. "Fuck, that's him. That's Samedi."

"Yeah, I know, but nothing we can do about that now."

"Yeah, you're right. Keep your eye on him until you can't anymore."

Detective Willis stood there watching the suspect. The man in the distance stared back at Frank, and after a while Frank started to feel uncomfortable. As the first of the EMT's arrived, Samedi, waved and faded away into the crowd. He was gone.

*   *   *   *

Detective Reingold and Detective Willis sat in the Captain's office waiting. Captain Oliver needed to talk to them about this morning's altercation. Three very reluctant witnesses backed up the detective's story of the events, so Tom wasn't going to be given desk duty, for now.

"Alright, guys," the Captain said when he walked into the office, "Tell me that you got more than a dead guy cooling off downstairs."

"Well," Frank started, "we saw our quarry. He knows that we know who he is now. He and his guardians, or whatever they want to think of themselves as, disappeared into the grounds, but we have an idea of where to look for his camp."

"Until this happened," the captain added in a chastising voice.

"Yeah, he might want to move, which is why I think we should get back there quickly."

"Okay," the captain said, "Get out there, but bring backup this time. I don't want a repeat of this morning. And get me something."

They were dismissed and the two detectives headed out to the patrol room to find some willing volunteers.

*   *   *   *

Detective Reingold was tossing through the small lean-to shelter that passed for Samedi's home. It was a lot nicer than most of the surrounding structures. Fear will get you things from the weaker and less fortunate. There were lots of pictures of people in one box, what looked to be a ton of tattooing equipment in others, and a calendar. There were four dates circled in red on the calendar and Tom thought that he recognized the dates, so he pulled out his pad to check.

"Hey, Frank. Get a load of this."

Frank walked over carrying a box of personal items that didn't look to be part of Samedi's usual things. "What you got?"

"The Monday that we got called in for the first one is circled. By the ME's calculating our second it would work to this date. There is one earlier and today is circled."

"Today?"

"Yeah."

"Fuck."

Tom thought for a moment, "Didn't you say there was some friend of yours with a similar case, might have been a freaky tattoo thing too? Call him and find out the date."

"On it," Frank said and stepped away to do just that.

Tom stood and was looking at the last wall. On a table there were candles in black and red and purple. Scattered haphazardly were bottles of rum and whiskey. Fresh and half smoked cigars littered the ashtray made from a skull. There were also many strange drawings that looked to Tom to be related to what he thought voodoo was all about. He called the religious man that he had visited with the other night and asked him to come down and take a look. The detectives needed to know what they were up against, and this was way out of their comfort zone for sure.

Frank came back and told Tom that the first date from the calendar was spot on. "That means that there is someone dying today or is already dead."

"Let's keep looking. Maybe we can find something that shows us the first deaths and that might help us find who is on the list now."

The two men gave up when at last they exhausted all the things that they could think of. Crime scene guys were taking the whole lot back to their lab to go through it with fine tooth combs. Maybe they could find something. The religious man had spent about thirty minutes telling the two detectives that they were looking for someone who truly believed that he was this Samedi God. The symbols were right, and all of the gathered accoutrements were right as well. He told them to be careful of his followers. If they thought that he was their God, they would die to protect him...period.

The sun was going down and Tom's stomach wouldn't stop rumbling. "Let's get something to eat and meet these guys back in the lab. Start fresh in an hour or so."

They left and made the long walk back to Tom's car. There they found a note on the windshield that said, 'DO NOT SLEEP'.

"Great," Frank said, "As if I didn't have a hard time sleeping as it was."

Tom crumpled up the note and shoved it into his pocket. "I'll sleep like a baby tonight, Frank, I'm not guilty of anything."

He lit up and drove them to their favorite diner which just happened to be a few blocks from the lab. They sat at the back booth and ordered coffee, lots of it, and food. Tom ordered the BLT on rye with mayo on the side, no French fries, but a serving of coleslaw. Frank went with the meatloaf platter, which came with mashed potatoes and vegetables. Frank being Frank of course, added a side dish of baked beans and to top it off some New York style cheesecake. Tom just shook his head. "I think I'll get you checked out for a tape worm."

They ate almost in silence, talking only about minor things like sports and cars and family. Tom finished long before Frank and sat back to enjoy the coffee. He closed his eyes to rest for a moment and was woken up by Frank. "Ready to go, Sleeping Beauty?"

Tom snapped up, "Sorry about that." He looked down at the now cleared off table and asked Frank, "How long was I out?"

"About twenty minutes. I didn't have the heart to wake you, but you drove." They laughed at that as they made their way out to the parking lot and on the short drive over to the lab.

Two hours later, with fresh coffee and most of the piles having been looked through, both of their cell phones went off almost simultaneously. They looked at each other knowing full well that this wouldn't be good news.

A few minutes later, they were on their way to the fresh crime scene knowing that this was going to be a long night.

*　　　　*　　　　*　　　　*

Detective Reingold wasn't shocked by much, but what he was looking at tonight got him deep inside. Frank had taken one look and threw up on the floor and had to leave. Tom stood there looking at the remains of a family man strapped into a sitting position. He also knew that the man they were hunting was more evil than anything he had encountered in his fifteen years on the force. Tom and the ME were slowly moving around the victim, both in awe and in a studious manner. They both had to see everything and learn from that what they could.

The man in the chair was Rich Foster. His wife had come home from work and found the grizzly scene and collapsed. Upon coming to, she crawled out of the home and called the police on her cell phone. A neighbor saw Mrs. Foster out on the lawn and rushed over to help, thinking that she might have been hurt. When the police had arrived, the detectives were called right in so Tom and Frank rushed over. Frank was now sitting out on the curb with a paramedic and probably driving him nuts, while Tom and the ME were trying to figure out what had happened.

Rich Foster had a large tattoo on his chest of a skeleton in leather riding a motorcycle. Rich was wearing a leather vest, unzipped to display the tattoo. Both of the victim's arms had had the skin and tissue eaten away, leaving a few tendons and fibers to hold what was remaining together. The atrocity stopped just below the shoulder, for the arms. Above the shoulders was another story all together. The man's head had gone through the same sort of stripping, down to the middle of the neck. The entire skull was exposed, no nose, face or any other identifying features. Both eyes were gone, and what was left of the neck was a disaster, half -eaten flesh, almost jelly-like at the edges, barely keeping the rest of the neck in shape.

He had been tied to the chair into the seated position. The bathtub looked to have been the scene of the stripping, or as Tom thought of it, dissolving. With what tools he had at the scene, Dr. Gold was sure that a lye substance had been used, something akin to sodium hydroxide or potassium hydroxide. Both would have done the job and the lab would have to determine which was used. Bits of wire could be seen throughout the visible skeletal remains, probably used to reinforce what was there to keep its shape, and shock value.

"Hey, Doc, how long would this like take? To dissolve someone like that?"

"The sad truth, Tom, is an entire body could be turned into a soup in less than eight hours with the right chemical and conditions."

"No shit?"

"Yeah, medical schools use a large vat of chemicals at a higher temperature, of course, to dispose of the cadavers used in training. After what the students put them through, they aren't much use for anything else after. That can take between something like six and ten hours, I think."

"Our guy didn't have that sort of time here." Tom put forth.

"No, he didn't, but he also only did a rather small portion of a body."

"Yeah, I guess."

The Doctor continued. "With boiling water and lye, I'm guessing that less than three hours might have been enough. Is there anything you can give me to help narrow down that timeline?"

Tom pulled out his notes. "According to the wife, she left him home in, uh, normal condition at around seven-forty-five this morning when she left for work. They spoke at lunchtime, around noon. Then, she found this when she got home. What a thing to come home to."

"I'll say." Dr. Gold wrote that down, "So in those five hours this happened. Close to what I had surmised."

The bathroom tub was a mess. A brownish thick fluid filled the tub about halfway. The killer had tried to drain it out, but the doctor was surmising that some part of the man remained large enough to have blocked the drain opening, and the killer sure as heck wasn't going to reach in to fix that. A kitchen chair was in the room and the doctor and Tom believed that Rich Foster had been tied to that chair and leveraged into the tub, head and arms to let the chemicals do their thing.

Bath towels littered the floor with bloody chunks of skin or flesh attached. The killer had probably used them to help stop the reaction and to clean up the bones to make the best presentation. The floor between the two rooms was scraped with two parallel lines which Tom was sure was caused by the killer dragging the chair back out with the body still in it.

Liquefied skin and flesh drops were hanging from the man's upper arm and neck. Tom was having a problem keeping his lunch down too, but remained steady until he had gotten all that he could. "Doc, we'll call you later to get whatever you have on the chemicals and…this."

Doctor Gold nodded and waved goodbye and went to collecting samples. Out on the curb, Frank was sipping water and waiting patiently for his partner. "You all right now?" Tom asked while stepping up alongside Frank and lighting up.

"Yeah, but what the fuck was that?" He shook his head. "That is not supposed to happen."

"You got that right, but it did, and now it's our job to catch the fucker responsible."

Detective Reingold got home just after midnight. He poured himself a double shot of gin and dropped into the recliner to sip at it in the dark and quiet. Now, he could finally come to grips with what had transpired today. He closed his eyes, but couldn't get the vision of Rich Foster to fade away. He accepted that it was going to be a sleepless night.

*　　　　*　　　　*　　　　*

A chill woke Tom up. He glanced at the clock on the wall to see that it was still a few minutes before one in the morning. Great, the damn pilot light must have gone out again. He got up and started to the closet to relight the heater but turned into the bathroom to empty his bladder instead. Priorities. When he was down on his knees igniting the little gas nozzle, he heard the floor creak behind him. He reached for his gun, but he came away empty, he had left it on the counter. He leapt up just in time to get tackled to the floor again. It was the two guys from the campgrounds. Tom kicked and punched, landing a few here and there, but he himself took the worst of it and finally felt the pull of darkness lifting him away from the fight.

Tom woke up in pain. His face hurt, his ribs hurt, and his chest was on fire. He opened his eyes and tried to jump away from what he saw but couldn't. He was tied tightly to a chair in this dining room. The two goons were seated at the table drinking Tom's good liquor and eating his food, while Samedi was tattooing Tom's chest. Tom looked down to see his face, and his hand holding a gun in his mouth. The back of Tom's head was shown very graphically being blown from his skull. There was blood squirting and flowing from his eyes and nose. Smoke was curling up and away from the barrel and ejector slot and a brass casing was tumbling away through the air.

Tom was impressed. This guy could actually draw and tattoo. "Is that what you're going to do to me?"

"Not tonight, my friend."

"I'm not your friend."

That brought a small smirk to Samedi's face which grew into a big smile and then a guttural laugh. "I guess that is true, Detective Reingold."

"Is this supposed to scare me? Me seeing this on my chest every time I take my shirt off?"

"No, Detective. What should scare you, is not knowing when you will do this, with my help. No, not tonight. Not tomorrow or even the day after. Start by counting weeks…maybe months. Then, you and I will sit again to make this true. This ink is very special. It has been blessed and so have I to do this work."

"You're not special. I hate to break it to you, but you're just a common psychopath."

"Oh, Sir, you are mistaken. There is nothing common about me." Samedi stood up and started chanting in a low rich voice. The two goons stood and slowly backed out of the room. Tom knew that he couldn't give into any fear that he might be holding inside. He truly believed that voodoo only worked on the weak minded, uneducated person. He wasn't one of those, so all he had to do is hold on.

The chanting grew in speed and volume, actually getting to the point where it was hard not to cover his ears. Did the lights flicker? Did Samedi grow larger? Tom trusted his gut. Silence popped back into the room with a vengeance. Tom opened his eyes and the room was empty. The goons were gone, Samedi and his equipment were gone. The tattoo wasn't. Tom looked down and his right hand had been untied. He used that to undo the bindings on his other limbs and slowly got out of the chair. His legs had gone to sleep. He must have been there longer than he thought he had. Looking up at the clock on the wall told him that it was just after seven in the morning.

Tom picked up his phone to call Frank and the crime lab, telling both what had happened and asking for help. He got to the front door to unlock it and then walked to the bathroom to see the tattoo that would be a constant reminder of this investigation, forever. There were some areas where there were little blood droplets, but most of the picture was just sore and slightly raised. The entire picture was about eight inches by eight inches across his left pectoral muscle. If it wasn't on his own body, Tom might have thought that the artist had been talented, something that he did not want attribute to this man.

Frank showed up first. "Holy shit, you okay?"

"As good as I can be."

"What the hell happened?"

Tom told him. Tom also moved to sit down in the living room, closer to the door because he wasn't feeling all that well. Maybe they had slipped him a drug or maybe he was having a reaction to the ink and pain, either way he didn't want to take any chances.

Frank left him and checked the rest of the apartment. Nothing was taken, not even Tom's service weapon or cell phone. Everything, other than the liquor and food that the invaders had used, was exactly how it should have been. The EMT's arrived and gave Tom a once over, finally giving the all clear just as Captain Jason Oliver arrived.

"How you holding up, Tom? I'm pulling you guys off of this now. I want all of your files on my desk first thing in the morning. Tom, you stay home. Frank, don't be late."

"Captain, that won't help," Tom said.

"And why is that?"

"This Samedi guy, says that he will be back sometime in a month or so to finish this. So, sitting out or staying in the game, won't mean anything to him."

"It will mean something to me if something bad happens to you in the meantime."

"I understand that Captain, but I want this guy, now more than ever."

"Another reason to keep you clear of the investigation. Do I make myself understood?"

Tom lowered his head and then stood up quickly, throwing the glass of water he was drinking against the wall. "Fuck!"

"Easy, Tom," Frank and the Captain said together.

Frank put his hand on Tom's shoulder and then turned to the Captain, "I got him, don't worry."

"I want those reports first thing."

"You'll get them. Thanks."

*   *   *   *

IV

The two detectives walked into the garage, the scene of the latest victim. Captain Oliver had called Frank to go pick up Tom and bring him to the scene. He didn't want him coming alone. It had been almost two weeks since Tom had had his run in with Samedi and things were quiet, until this morning. An auto body repair shop owner was opening up when he stumbled across the body. He immediately called it in. After seeing what was there, Captain Oliver called Frank.

"Captain," Tom called when his eyes adjusted to the dark interior of the building, "What's going on?"

"What's going on is that a body was found this morning. A tattoo that the ME says might have been done around the same time as yours was mimicked in this death."

"I thought that I was off of this case?"

"Don't be an asshole, Tom. I called you because you are on the case, and because you knew this individual."

Tom and Frank looked at each other, both taken aback by that information. "Who was it?" Tom asked.

"I believe you knew him as Jimmy 'The Head'."

"Fuck, God damn it." Tom was visibly shaken and Frank, though shocked had more concern about his partner.

"How…how did it…show me the tattoo. I know that you have scene photos."

Captain Oliver pulled a folder off of the table and handed it to Tom. Tom took a deep breath and opened the folder with Frank looking closely over his shoulder. Tom snapped his eyes shot, thinking about the poor man Jimmy. Jimmy had been dealt a bad hand from the get-go and life never let up. He had been abused as a child, had spent time in and out of juvie, or the Juvenile Detention Center, and then regular prison. He couldn't hold down a real job and had been homeless as far back as Tom knew, and now this had happened to him. If Samedi had captured Jimmy and tattooed him as he had done to Tom, he could empathize.

The first picture was of the tattoo. It showed a body, well more accurately a torso, with the limbs removed and spaced out. It looked like what a kid's doll would look like when the arms and legs had been popped out of their sockets. The exaggerated shaped head left little doubt as to the victim's identity. Beyond that, each of the limbs had been separated at the joints; upper arm from forearm, thigh from shin. Tom closed his eyes and felt so many emotions running through his mind. Feelings of hatred toward Samedi, pity for Jimmy, as well as empathy, and revenge to name a few. All of them were fighting for the control of Tom's now fragile mind.

He flipped to the next picture and saw what he had expected and braced his mind for. Jimmy had been dismembered and left spread out across the garage floor. As he flipped through the pictures, each from different angles or distances, Tom felt tears welling up in his eyes.

Tom got up and went inside to get brought up to speed. He could see the large blood stains on the concrete floor. If you connected the dots, so to speak, you could see how the body had been positioned. The pictures showed that the dismembering had been done roughly and crudely. Tom saw that there was a bloody machete lying on the floor to the body's left, and a gore covered pneumatic hammer lying near the head of the victim. "Hey, Doc, what do you have for me?"

Doctor Gold walked him through how he thought it went down by the blood flow and positioning of the parts. "Tom, I understand that you knew the victim, are you ready for this?"

"I'm a professional, Doc, tell me."

"Well, with what I see, it looks like the legs were removed first near the hip. The extensive bruising on the upper arms and shoulders indicate that he was alive and fighting to get away when this, and I'm sorry that I don't have another word for it, brutality had started."

Tom closed his eyes.

"The blood loss would have been major, and he wouldn't have survived long afterwards…"

"That's good."

"It's hard to say if the arms were removed before or after the legs had been broken down further, but I am sure that he was deceased before that had happened."

"You sure?"

"Yeah, the blood flow was so minimal where the separation occurred. I'm sorry, Tom."

Tom stood there silently looking at the carnage spread out before him. Yeah, he had known the victim. Yeah this was bad. His mind was racing. Why couldn't I have protected him? How did those guys get the drop on me? I let the fuckers get away.

He heard a voice from his left and turned to see Captain Oliver asking, "Are you okay, Tom?"

"Yeah," a pause, "No." He handed the folder back to the captain and turned and started walking out of the garage, "I gotta go."

Frank followed him out to the street, "I'll take you home."

"No need, I'll be fine. Go take care of this, will ya?"

Frank watched him walking toward the bus stop a block away. There was a small kiosk with two people already waiting. Frank could remember the last time that he and Tom had spoken to Jimmy. He had just been assaulted and his face was a mess. He had given the detectives enough information to go looking on their own, but isolated himself from the actual scene. Apparently not, thought Frank. Either way, the man didn't deserve what had happened to him.

*　　　　*　　　　*　　　　*

Detective Tom Reingold strode though the campgrounds on a mission. He went directly to the place where they had seen Samedi the last time. The lean-to and the surrounding camps were gone. Frantically, Tom spun and ran through the darkening landscape, desperate for a glimpse. After a while, Tom slowed. He was panting for breath, and then crying.

He dropped to his knees. Tom had been a cop a long time and this was the first time that he felt himself losing it.

He looked up at the sky and screamed, "SAMEDI!!"

Immediately cats and dogs howled, and birds took off, frightened, the flapping wings carrying them away from the terrifying sound. Tom slowly sank down and fell back onto his ass to sit there. Tears filled his eyes and ran down his cheeks. He reached for the cell phone and called for Frank to come get him.

On the trip back to Tom's home, Frank asked, "Want to tell me what's going on, Pal? That was a crazy stunt you pulled and could have easily gotten yourself killed."

"Yeah, I know. It's just that…Jimmy didn't deserve…I want this mother fucker."

"We'll get him. It's only a matter of time, but you gotta relax. Let's work together. You can't be flying off half-cocked like that again."

"All right, all right, I get it. I'm sorry."

When the two detectives walked into Tom's living room, the lights went out, and they were attacked violently. The two men fought the attackers the best that they could but were soon overwhelmed.

*　　　　　*　　　　　*　　　　　*

Tom opened his eyes. He saw the two goons sitting again at his table drinking. This shit has got to stop, he thought. Samedi was sitting patiently facing him, his chair pulled around the end of the table. Tom looked down. His shins were bound to the chair and his left arm was numb. Glancing at it, he saw that the bindings were a little tight and he yelled at his inner self to relax. He felt weight in his right hand and looked there to see his service weapon firmly in his grasp.

"Where's Frank?" Tom asked with a raspy voice.

Samedi answered, "He is in a dreamland in the other room. No need for you to worry about him now. Your time and my time has arrived. Do you remember our last conversation?"

Tom stretched his shoulders and neck and could see Frank lying on the floor, and after a moment saw that he was at least breathing which meant that he was alive.

"Yeah, I remember it, asshole."

One of the goons started to get up, but a slight wave of Samedi's hand sat him right back down.

"I see you got them trained pretty well there. They sit up and beg too?"

"Now, now, Mr. Reingold, there is no need for that sort of talk. You and I have some unfinished business and it is time now to conclude with that."

Samedi reached across to Tom and ripped open his shirt. Pulling and tearing at it until it was almost all off of him. "Do you remember what I draw for you here?"

"How could I forget? I see it every fucking day and what I feel is hatred for you!" Tom remembered the pistol in his hand and quickly raised it to Samedi's face. Again, the goons tried to intervene and once more were dismissed with a flip of the wrist.

Samedi looked at the raised weapon, closed his eyes and started chanting. As he did, Samedi raised his hands, felt for Tom's extended arm and slowly, methodically guided it so that the barrel was inside of Tom's mouth. When Tom felt the barrel on his tongue, his index finger started to tighten against the trigger.

Tom tried to turn his head, but couldn't. He tried to drop the gun, but couldn't. He was watching Samedi. The closed eyes, the strong fingers and grip, the chanting. From the side, Tom noticed that the goons had started backing out of the room just as they had done the last time.

"Tom…Tom…no…fight it…"

Tom heard Frank off to his right, but couldn't turn. He tried again to pull the gun out of his mouth, but couldn't. The index finger tightened again, and Tom watched the hammer. It had been pulled back when the slide had jacked a round into the chamber. When the hammer moved, it would be all over. Tom wasn't even sure if he would see it happen. Tighter. Tighter.

"Tom…no…"

Samedi opened his eyes and smiled. The loud explosion of a gun going off broke the tension. Tom looked at his hand and the hammer was still down. Samedi slowly dropped forward with blood blossoming across his chest. Tom looked over toward Frank. He was still on the floor, but holding his weapon up towards the room and there was smoke rising from the barrel's opening. Tom pulled the gun from his mouth just as the two goons rushed back in. Tom shot them both, ending the standoff.

It took Tom almost fifteen minutes to remove the bindings and get out of the chair. He rushed to Frank who had multiple stab wounds. "I got ya buddy, hang in there." He rushed to the bathroom and came back with towels and immediately applied pressure. "Here, hold this...tight."

He reached for his cell and called in the ambulance and for back up. Then he called the Captain.

"Frank, hold on will ya. And hey...thanks."

Frank looked up at him. "Thought I lost you there, Pal."

"Nah...the smoking will get me before someone like that."

That brought a smile to Frank's face followed by a grimace. "Don't make me laugh, damn it."

*   *   *   *

Three days later, Frank was wheeled out of the hospital to the curb as he waited for Tom to get the car. Once they had pulled away from the curb, Frank said, "Thank God that's over. I couldn't eat any more of that shit if there was a gun to my head. Oh shit, man...sorry. I didn't mean..."

Tom just looked over at him. "Diner, or pub?"

"Diner."

The following afternoon the toxicology report was in. Tom had been given a mild dose of a hallucinogen which allowed the manipulation by Samedi. As it turned out, Samedi was a local man, Lawrence White, and was wanted in two states for pan handling, robbery, drug and weapon possession, and assorted other crimes. The two goons were just that. They were two local ex-gang thugs hired by Samedi to protect him from rivals and the police.

Captain Oliver broke it down to the two detectives. "This was way beyond anything I had dealt with in a long time, and you two got it done, almost. You also almost got yourselves killed. Two weeks on the desk, and three days a week with Doctor Robinson. No sign off from her, you stay riding the bench. Got it?"

They agreed and went back to work, answering the phones and writing reports. At ten thirty Frank said to Tom, "Ready for some lunch?"

"You drive, I'm drinking."

"Drinking?"

Tom was up and tossing his jacket on and walking away, "Yeah, they got the best coffee around and I'm carrying a few back. You coming?"

"Coffee and cigarettes and yet he worries about my bacon and egg intake. Wait up."

*   *   *   *

"Willis…yes Captain…no why?…I'll try him and call you back."

Frank called his partner Tom Reingold six times in as many minutes. He never doesn't pick up. After calling the captain, Frank was out and, in the car, and speeding through traffic with his blue and red lights flashing, mounted in his grill.

When Frank arrived at Tom's home there were already two other squad cars, an ambulance and the coroners van. "Fuck!" Frank yelled as he came to a halt on the neighbor's lawn.

As he was headed for the house, Doctors Gold, the ME was coming out. "Whoa, Frank, you don't want to go in there."

"He's my partner get of the way."

"Frank." The way the ME said it froze Frank in his stride. "There's nothing to do in there."

"Yeah, there is. He is…or was…my partner. I gotta do this. For him…and for me."

Doctor Gold stepped aside, and Frank walked into the home. Captain Oliver was there talking to the other detectives and crime scene technicians. He looked up and saw Frank. Walking over he said, "Frank, you really should go home. I got this. We'll treat him right, okay?"

"I gotta see, Captain."

The Captain led Frank to the dining room. There he found Tom, sitting in the chair, his service pistol lying on the floor on his right side and a very big messy red spray on the wall behind him. The reality of the death right above the exposed image etched onto Tom's chest those few weeks ago. Tom's vacant eyes were staring straight ahead at a picture of Jimmy 'The Head' lying on the table in front of him. There was also a half-full bottle of good scotch and a glass with a little remaining in it as well.

"I'm sorry, Frank."

"Yeah, Jason, me too."

THE END

Birthright

"What the hell is wrong with you, woman?" the irate drunken man yelled.

His wife cowering against the counter whimpered, "I'm…sorry."

The punch caught the woman in the side of the face and her knees collapsed, she grabbed a hold of the countertop to keep from falling to the floor.

"Leave her alone," Michael yelled at his father. At sixteen he was still too weak to defend his mother properly, but he'd had enough. He swung his fist and hit his father while stepping between the two adults.

The father reeled back. "You little fucker," he hissed, right before beating the living hell out of Michael.

When he awoke, Michael found his mother, with a black eye and swollen lip, taking care of his bruises and cuts.

"Why is he like that, Mom?"

"Your father is a good man, but he has this terrible anger inside, Michael. He got beat by his father, who got beat by his. It's just who they are."

"Well, I'm not going to do that," Michael said. He touched his face and winced. "Ever."

Michael Ostrog and his family lived in a small rural town where this sort of thing didn't raise any eyebrows. What happened between a man and his family was between them, unless of course it led to a killing. It wasn't long after the next beating that Michael and his mother left the father and moved back to her mother's home. It was close enough to keep the friends that she had had, while just a little too far for a drunken man to make the effort travelling to.

*   *   *   *

"Mike!"

"Yeah."

"Need you to pull a double. That bastard, Franklin called in sick again."

"Damn it, Boss, that's the third time this week."

"Yeah, well do you want it, or not?"

"Yeah, yeah. I'll stay." Michael didn't mind staying most of the time since the time-and-a-half made his check at the end of the week much fatter. It had been ten years since he had left home and moved to the city. After months of menial jobs and scratching out a living, Michael had come to the docks and had worked there ever since. He was respected as a hard worker and tough guy. Nobody fucked with Michael. The last few guys who thought they could handle him went alone to the hospital to have broken and ruptured things repaired. He was friendly enough when left to his own devices, just don't cross that line.

Tomorrow was Sunday and he could sleep in. Michael lived alone and answered to no one. When he did wake up, he tossed a frozen breakfast into the microwave oven and sat in front of the television to watch the sports updates. He pushed the remains aside and picked up the phone to call his mother. He had promised to come up the next weekend to go through his father's possessions. The man had died by taking on a tree with his old car. The tree had won.

Michael hated everyone, except his mother. He hated having to be polite in public situations when the asshole didn't deserve it. He wanted to beat the shit out of so many people and fought it every day. That's when he knew that his genetic material did indeed come from his father.

*   *   *   *

Going through his father's house brought back very few good memories for Michael. His mother seemed better for have coming. He had called ahead to have a dumpster provided into which most of the contents of the house would be going. The task at first seemed daunting, but the physical labor didn't bother Michael at all. It was good to see his mother too; it had been a while. They talked. Michael's mother seemed relieved that this dark part of her life was over for good. She didn't have to look over her shoulder anymore. Michael on the other hand, felt nothing.

On a shelf in the garage, Michael found an old tin cigar box. He opened it and saw pictures and letters, very old pictures and letters. They reminded Michael of the ones you saw in old news footage of

New York, or those of the Civil War. Michael reached to toss it into the pail he was using to transport junk to the dumpster, but caught himself. Something made him want to take it home and look at them closer. There could be something valuable there.

Two weeks later Michael saw the box in the trunk of his car and brought it into the house with the groceries and dropped it on the table. After eating dinner, he sat at the table to go through its contents. The pictures had names and dates written on the back. Michael was looking at pictures of his grandfather and grandmother that he never knew he had. He was surprised when he saw his name on the back of one from nineteen-oh-five. His great- great-grandfather. They shared the same name.

Michael also found documents of marriage, death and letters back and forth to strange names. One in particular caught his eye. He read the letter may times that night, still unable to grasp what it was implying.

*   *   *   *

Detective John Summers stood in the rain and watched as the Coroner, Doctor William Eastwood, reviewed what was in front of him. A woman had been killed last night, the beginning of the holiday weekend. Detective Summers was also thinking that his wife would be pissed when he had to tell her that he had caught a case and wouldn't be around much over the next few days when their children were in town.

Doctor Eastwood looked up at the detective, "Well, she's missing four or five teeth, and there's a small laceration of the tongue. There is also a bruise along the right-side lower part of the jaw on her face. I'm thinking that it might have been caused by a blow, like from a fist, but with a circular bruise on the left side of the face, the set might have been inflicted by the pressure of the fingers."

"So, she was grabbed by the face. Was it to hold her to pull the teeth out? Or do you think they were knocked out by a punch or other impact?"

"Hard to say until I get her on the table. Remember, everything I'm telling you now is preliminary."

"Gotcha."

"On the left side of the neck just below the jaw, there's a four-inch-long incision starting just below the ear. On the same side, about an inch lower, and commencing about one inch in front of it, was a circular incision that ends about three inches below her right jaw. Damn, it completely severed all the tissues down to her vertebrae. The jugular and carotids on both sides were severed. It's about eight inches in length I would guess…"

"Damn, this guy really wanted her dead."

"Yeah, ya think? My opinion right now, the cuts were caused by a long-bladed knife which was used with great violence. Not a lot of blood on the breast or the clothes. So, she was lying down when it was done to her."

"Is that what killed her?" the detective asked.

"Again, hard to say until I get her on the table. There are five or six cuts across her abdomen all of which had been caused by a knife which had been used viciously and in a downwards direction. The injuries look like they might have been done by a lefthanded person. Very jagged, and it looks to me like all the injuries had been caused by the same instrument."

"A big knife or one of those fucking box cutter things?"

"No, definitely a long blade. Maybe something a butcher would use."

"Gotcha. Any ID on her?"

"Yeah," the doctor reached for the purse and opened it. He pulled out the wallet, "her name's Nichols, Mary Nichols. Uh, thirty-eight years old. From Brooklyn."

The detective made his notes. "And she was killed last night, which was, August thirty-first, right?"

"Yeah. And what a shame, she looks like she was well off."

"Then what the hell was she doing in this neighborhood?"

When they were through, Detective Summers made his way to Brooklyn to ask the neighbors about Mary. None of them knew why she was in the worst part of town. She usually wouldn't go there. She had a nice apartment and lived probably just above her means. The detective had a thought that maybe Mary had needed money and was hitting the streets. Something that area of Redhook was known for.

*　　　　*　　　　*　　　　*

Michael went to the library to use the computers there to do some research. He needed to know more about the names and people in these letters. He spent three hours on the internet pouring over the information that the search engines popped up. He couldn't understand what he was reading. It had to be a joke or something. He wouldn't put that past his father, but something nagged at him. He honestly didn't think his father was smart enough to pull it off, so it had to be real.

The names were real, and the letters seemed genuine. Two of the letters in particular were apparently first drafts of the letters that were eventually sent to Scotland Yard. There were line outs and additions. When Michael saw one of those letters, posted from eighteen-eighty-eight in its final form he sat back shocked. It had been sent to a News Agency of the time and was printed in many of the local news papers hoping to get help from the public in finding a killer that was terrorizing the area.

Michael couldn't believe what he was reading. On one hand it would explain a little about the men in his family line. On the other hand, he could be sitting on a pot of gold. Who could he see to find out about its validity and price? Michael didn't have those sorts of connections, and he certainly didn't want to just go to the police.

Two more hours of surfing the net and Michael had written down a few names and phone numbers that he felt he could turn to in his search for answers. On his way home, Michael stopped at his favorite bar and had a few drinks. While sitting on a stool in the corner he came up with a better plan.

*   *   *   *

"Hey, Doc," Detective John Summers called out as he walked towards where the coroner stood over a new body. Detective Summers had gotten the call a little over an hour ago at six-thirty and made his way over. He took a sip from his coffee cup and dropped it into the bucket set up for the police to use so that they wouldn't contaminate the crime scene.

"Mornin', Detective." The doctor finished writing something in his notes and met the detective. "This one is bad. She's cut up and some of her insides are missing, I think."

"You think?"

"Hey, until I get her on the table and see what's there, and what isn't, it's hard to tell. Right now, whatever is there is spread all over the room."

"Shit, and I just ate breakfast." Detective Summers pulled on the booties and gloves provided and followed the doctor back to the body. "Oh, man, you weren't kidding." The sight in front of the detective was worse than what he had thought it would be. "What can you tell me? Give me something to start with, okay?"

"It will be guess work, but she's in rigor and might have been strangled to start. The swollen tongue indicates that in some cases. The severe lacerations across the throat and the signs of blood high on the wall here indicate that she was still alive when the major arteries were severed. Her abdomen has been opened and you can see the intestines draped across her chest and shoulders. Again, I can't tell for sure, but he might have taken some of her internal organs with him. I can tell you more later this afternoon."

"Thanks. Any ID?"

"Yeah, her purse is over there and seems intact."

"Whoa, what's a girl with a thousand-dollar Coach purse doing in this neighborhood?"

"You're the detective, Detective."

"Ann Chapman it says here. Forty-three years of age from Brooklyn. So, we have another well to do woman, brutalized down here. Does that make it serial?"

"For a serial, Detective, there has to be three…"

"Great. I'll see you later."

"After three I should have something to give you."

"Gotcha." Detective Summers pulled off his gloves and booties and headed towards the closest place to get good coffee. It was going to be a long day.

*　　　　*　　　　*　　　　*

"Holy shit!" the man said. "Do you know what you have here?"

Michael looked at the guy. "If I fucking knew, why would I be here?"

"Yeah... right, anyway, this all looks like the real thing. The paper is right, the ink bleed, the aging. Holy shit, man." The man was examining the letters under a special light and with a loupe.

"So, is it valuable?" Michael wanted to know.

"Tell me again, where did you get it?"

"I found it cleaning out my father garage. Those are my grandfathers."

"No fucking way." The man looked Michael over. "For real, man?"

"Yeah, so?"

"Oh yeah, I know people that will pay real good money for this stuff."

"How good?"

"Honestly, I would guess in the upper six figures to seven."

Michael sat back. This was the second man to tell him the same thing. He now knew he wasn't getting played. "What would it take to set up an auction for it? You know, like an off the books auction like you see in the movies for this stuff?"

"You said it man, that's in the movies. In real life, it's a little harder. Not impossible, but tougher. Shady people like legitimacy. If they think they're getting ripped off, it can get real bad real fast."

Michael picked up the box with the papers and told the guy to call him when he thought he could set something up. Michael put the box in a plastic bag and stuffed it under the driver's seat when he got back to the car, which he had parked four blocks away.

*　　　　*　　　　*　　　　*

Detective Summers walked into the morgue and found Doctor Eastwood just finishing up. "I miss anything?"

"Detective, you're right on time."

"What can you tell me now?"

"Well, for starters, this is one sick individual. Having knocked the woman down, the killer then cut her throat which led to massive bleeding and a quick death. Again, the cuts were made right to left, so a lefthanded person is probable. There are deep gauges in the spinal bones, or vertebrae, indicating that he had tried a little bit to sever the head from the body."

"What made him stop?"

"My guess is that he had the wrong type of blade. To go through the bones, you would need a heavy thick blade. It looks like all the injuries are done with a very sharp knife with a thin narrow blade, and it must have been maybe six to eight inches in length, maybe a little longer."

"Like a bayonet or something like a short sword?"

"No, not like that. This would be an instrument like something a medical man would use for post-mortem purposes, but we don't use or carry anything like that. It might be something used by a slaughter man, or a hunter for his field dressing."

"Okay, at least that's something. Did he take anything like you suspected?"

"Yes, he did. As you saw, her abdomen had been entirely laid open. Her intestines had been severed from their mesenteric attachments and placed on the shoulder."

"Yeah, I remember."

"This guy then removed the uterus and its appendages with the upper portion of the vagina and the posterior two thirds of the bladder. I couldn't find any trace of these parts. And, the incisions were cleanly cut, he avoided the rectum, and divided the vagina low enough to avoid injury to the cervix uteri. He must have had some knowledge of anatomical or pathological examinations to be able to secure the pelvic organs with one sweep of the knife."

"So maybe a doctor or surgeon?"

"Or veterinarian for that matter, or a butcher."

"That's a lot of people in a city this big, Doc."

"Listen, I couldn't have done this to her in under fifteen or twenty minutes. He was either there a long time or this guy is lucky."

Detective Summers looked over his notes. "So, we have a Mary Nichols and now an Ann Chapman. Both having no business where they were found."

A Medical Assistant who was cleaning up after the doctor asked, "What were those names again? Did you say Mary Nichols and Ann Chapman?"

The coroner and the detective looked at the man. Detective Summers said, "Yeah, those are the names. Do they mean something to you?"

"Well, I think those are pretty famous names in the killer world. Hang on a second and I'll check." He walked to the desk and sat behind the computer and started typing while the coroner and detective followed to watch over this shoulder.

A few keystrokes later, Detective Summers blew out some air and said, "No way."

The assistant scrolled down to where the article talked about the victims. The names were the same and now the three men saw that the atrocities visited upon these women had been done before, in eighteen-eighty-eight to be precise. That killer had never been caught, but everybody knew his name.

Detective Summers said, "Jack the fucking Ripper?"

"It appears that we have a copycat with a lot of time on his hands." Doctor Eastwood stated. "This guy has seen this and read it and studied it."

"He probably carries a list with him to make sure he gets it right." Detective Summers thought out loud. "Hey, by the way, what's your interest in this?" he asked the assistant.

"I'm studying to be a Forensic Pathologist, and this is one of the best unsolved cases out there. I was reading about it a few weeks ago. When you said the names, I was thinking, what? Did they just say that? I was thinking that I must have misheard you guys."

"Okay, great. Now, can you print all this shit out for me?" the detective asked.

"Sure."

Five minutes later Detective Summers was speeding across town with the lights on to get to the office. He now had a lead. His mind was whirling. Jack the Ripper is one of the most famous of all killers in modern times. If this bad guy wanted to be him or to try and out do him, then the detective was thinking that he would have his hands full real fast. To catch this guy, he would have to get out in front of him. He had on the seat next to him a large pile of papers to get a look into the guys mind. He only had to get in, see where it would lead, and get there first, and it had to be fast. He knew just the guy to ask for help.

*　　　　*　　　　*　　　　*

Michael Ostrog finally got a call from one of the antique guys. He had left them with copies of the documents to get the interest up, but knew he had to do more, so he spent the whole weekend searching the internet for what he needed. He had to find a woman with the right name, like the first two, but it was impossible. The name wasn't in the New York area at all. He also wanted the media to get wind of what was happening, and once it had, the prices and interest in the pieces he had would soar. With the letters burning in his mind, Michael made a decision and mailed one to the detective on the case. He had called the police, telling them that he was a family member of the first girl and needed to talk to the detective. He had lied his ass off but got the detective's name and sent him the letter.

*   *   *   *

  Detective Summers opened the letter and grimaced. He set it down and called the Crime Scene Technicians. Once they had it sealed, he picked it up to read. Detective Robert Archer was there with him. He was a historian and knew about all things in the detective world, both real and fiction. Bob knew everything. He had been intrigued by the call he had received from Detective Summers earlier in the day. Now, going over the material, and with this new turn of events, he was convinced. Whoever was doing this was indeed a Jack the Ripper wannabe, and that made him dangerous.

  "This is the real deal, John," Detective Archer said. "But, I am curious about where this guy came across this. An original would have had to been handed down in the family of either the police at the time, or, if I can even say it aloud, from the Ripper himself."

"The Ripper left this in a will or something?"

"Well, he was never caught. Some people surmised that he fled England to the states about the turn of the century. Any belongings he had could have come into the possession of anyone he came in contact with."

"But why hide it so long?"

"Well, either they didn't know what they had, or this is someone just coming into ownership of it."

"Shit, either way it doesn't shorten the list."

"Afraid not."

Detective Summers sat back and thought about that. "Well, if it is a descendant, we have to go over that list of suspects on that website to narrow down the possibilities."

"Agreed, and I'll make a few calls."

Detective Summers then asked, "What's the names of the other victims. We have to find them too."

Detective Archer answered him, "The next murder was actually a double. At least the records say that they were both done by the Ripper."

"Great."

"One is named Elizabeth Stride and the other was Catharine Eddowes, I think. Both killed on September thirtieth."

Detective Summers was busily typing the names into the DMV Database. "Okay, so we have, what, two weeks?"

"There about, if he keeps to the schedule."

"I'm thinking that he has too. These twisted fuckers have no choice." After a moment he added, "Shit, there's no women with either of these names, not even close."

"Then he'll be playing a new game."

"Great. Just when we get a look at the script, he gets a new writer."

*   *   *   *

Michael spent the better part of the day pissed off. He had searched the internet and there were no women with the names for the next victim. When he got home, he kicked and punched a hole in the wall. What was he going to do? He needed to find a woman with that name and all he could find was an old man.

Michael jumped into the car and went to visit his mother. After eating a dinner that she had cooked for him, they sat in the living room and watched the news. When the story of the two dead women came up, Michael's mother said, "That is so sad, those women."

"Why sad?" Michael asked.

"Because those things shouldn't have happened to those nice women."

"It would have been okay to happen if they were whores?" Michael asked.

"Of course not, Michael, but we both know what happened to them."

Michael was shocked. "What are you saying, Mom?"

"I knew about the letters, Michael and knew all the names forwards and back. I prayed every night that you wouldn't go down this path. I also searched your father's house for anything about them, but I guess you found it instead and kept it to yourself."

"You knew?"

"Yes." Michael's mother was crying. "I knew. I'm not proud of it, but yes, I knew."

"So, what should I do, Mom? If you know, how long do you think before the police do?"

"Not long, Michael. Not long."

Michael stood up and went to get another beer. When he returned his mother was looking up at him. "I will still love you, Michael, and I understand."

Michael bent down to kiss his mother and after doing so, grabbed her head and twisted it roughly and quickly to face the other direction. The loud snapping sound seemed to echo through the room. A tear came up in Michael's eye and he brushed it away with the back of his hand. He sat and finished his beer and stroked his mother's hand.

*   *   *   *

The desk phone rang. "Detective Summers here…yes…yes…really?…I'll be right down."

Jim MacDonald was waiting for him when he walked into the office. Jim was the Medical Assistant that first mentioned the Ripper connection. "I ran a lot of the names off of the Ripper site and saw that most of the suspects had died in prison soon after those dates. Most didn't have families. But one guy, a Michael Ostrog seems to have disappeared in the early nineteen hundreds."

"Disappeared?"

"Yeah, there seems to be no mention of him after that, in Europe."

"In Europe?"

"Yeah, but guess who emigrated here in nineteen-oh-five?"

"This Michael Ostrog?"

"His family still lives about an hour north of the city."

"No way?"

"Here's the address."

The detective looked at the paper in front of him and saw two addresses. One was upstate and one was in the city. "What's this one?"

"A son, or grandson, or whatever, but there isn't much on him in the system."

The detective thanked Jim and left to get some backup.

*   *   *   *

When Detective Summers and Detective Johnson pulled up to the curb at the house, they saw that the car parked in the driveway was registered to the man they were looking to talk to, the son who had moved to the city. No one had been home at that address earlier, and now they knew why.

The two men approached the door and knocked. They heard the thumping of running feet and crashing inside the house. Detective Summers stood back, and it took two kicks from his heavy feet to knock in the door. There was banging at the back of the house and Detective Johnson went that way while

Detective Summers stopped in the living room. The smell drew him. What he saw was terrifying.

Mrs Ostrog had been butchered. Her throat was cut, and she had been gutted like the last victim. Her intestines were on display around her shoulders and there were other parts of her insides lying on the floor. Blood was pooling under and around the chair she was sitting in. It was one of those old rockers and was still shifting eerily forward and back in the semi-dark room. Detective Summers spun and ran towards the back when he heard the two gun shots.

Two men were standing and wrestling in the kitchen when he got there. The gun was lying on the other side the room on the floor. Detective Summers yelled, "Michael, stop!"

The man didn't. Detective Summers shot his weapon into the ceiling as a warning and all it seemed to do was piss off the bigger assailant. Michael punched Detective Johnson hard in the face and Detective Summers saw blood fly. He aimed his weapon at the man and yelled again. "Michael, stop it. Don't make me do this!"

When Michael raised his fist again, Detective Summers Shot him three times. Two of the shots hit him in the chest and one in the side of the neck. He was dead before he hit the floor. Detective Johnson had suffered a broken nose, but that was all, unless you count the blow to his ego.

There was a copy of the coroner's report lying on the floor next to the deceased mother. Michael had decided to use her for the third victim and was recreating the scene from the descriptions found there. Detective Summers couldn't understand how a son could do that to his mother. He walked out of the house with blood on his hands and on his shoes. The sticky sucking sounds followed him down the front walk.

*   *   *   *

The old tin box had been found under the front seat of the car and its contents were sent to Scotland Yard for verification and for their safe keeping. No one knew for sure whether or not the original Michael Ostrog was the Ripper or if he had just found the letters some other way. There was nothing to say that the letters hadn't been fabricated after the events by the eighteen-eighty-eight Michael to become part of one of his schemes. He had spent time in English and French prisons for petty crimes and no one truly believed that he was the Ripper, and this new information only added to the mystique.

With their case solved, Detective Summers took Detective Johnson and Jim MacDonald out for drinks. They had both helped him and he wanted to show his appreciation. Inside, Detective Summers was sure that Michael had been the descendant of the Ripper. It only made sense if the papers had been handed down father to son, father to son. Somehow, the two-thousand-thirteen Michael Ostrog had seen them as his birthright.

THE END

TITLE	DATE WRITTEN
My Summer Vacation	9/11/08
The First Date	9/02/08
Bless me Father	12/01/09
The Goodbye Tear	12/24/09
Killer	11/28/10
The Future and Past Collide	9/03/10
The Next Leve	11/02/10
Krandall	5/19/11
Lost and Found	3/10/13
Illuminator	4/30/13
Bad Ink	12/10/15
Birthright	5/19/13

ABOUT THE AUTHOR

George Gross III has been writing since he started junior high school. He read a lot as a child, encouraged by his family and a few close friends, also readers. Even back then he read across most genres covering everyone from Shakespeare, to Agatha Christie, to Dashiell Hammett, to JRR Tolkien and Robert Heinlein. He has spent time in law enforcement, served in the military, travelled extensively as a musician and has worked for over thirty years in the engineering environment. These short stories were written over many years and George was finally talked into putting out these three collections (with more to follow).

Made in the USA
Middletown, DE
18 June 2021

42668563R00146